STORIES FROM EAST HIGH #4

CRUNCH TIME

By N.B. Grace

Based on the Disney Channel Original Movie
High School Musical, written by Peter Barsocchini

Bath New York Singapore Hong Kong Cologne Delhi Melbourne

This edition published by Parragon in 2008
Parragon
Queen Street House
4 Queen Street
Bath BA1 1HE, UK

Copyright © 2007 Disney Enterprises, Inc.

ISBN 978-1-4075-3133-5

Printed in UK

CHAPTER ONE

It was only 8:30 in the morning, but an air of nervousness already filled Ms Darbus's tutor-room. Gabriella Montez chewed her lip and flipped through her calculus textbook, doing one last-minute check that she had memorized all the formulas that were going to be on today's big test.

Three rows back, Troy Bolton had his eyes closed, but he wasn't nodding off. Instead, he was mentally going over the new drill that the basketball team had learned two days ago. He was going to lead practice today, and he wanted to make sure that he knew the moves backwards and forwards.

Two rows across, Sharpay Evans passed her brother, Ryan, a note with yet another idea about how they could improve the dance routine they were creating for the school's next talent contest. True, it was months away, but it was never too early to start working on perfection! Ryan read the note and then looked over at his sister in awe. Once again, Sharpay had demonstrated why she was destined to be world-famous by the time she was twenty-five. He mouthed the word, "Brilliant!" and she nodded smugly.

Ms Darbus looked out at the class and sighed. She had never seen a more distracted group of students since – well, to be fair, since yesterday's tutor group. She was about to call the class to order when the speaker on the wall emitted a loud screech.

Everyone jumped, even though they should

have known this was coming. Principal Matsui was completely incapable of handling any kind of sound system. Every morning started with a painful blast of feedback.

Another loud screech. Troy groaned, Ryan put his head on his desk and Sharpay put her hands over her ears. Ms Darbus rolled her eyes and made a mental note to once again offer to have one of her stagehands teach Principal Matsui the basics of volume control.

Finally, Principal Matsui managed to get his mike to work. His voice boomed out over the PA system.

"Good morning, East High School!" he cried. "It's now time for the morning announcements!"

In the back row, Zeke Baylor let his head fall back against the wall and closed his eyes. Unlike his friends, he wasn't distracted by looming tests, basketball drills or dance routines, and he had found that the morning announcements always offered a good opportunity to get a little shuteye. After all, so many of them were about totally boring topics, like—

"Remember the SAT tutoring sessions start this week!" the principal said. "They'll be held on Tuesdays and Thursdays for an hour after school and they'll be led by other students! Not only will you learn a lot, but I'm sure that you'll make new friends and have a lot of fun!"

Studying for the SATs – fun?

Zeke opened his eyes just long enough to look over at his team-mate, Chad Danforth, with an expression of exaggerated horror. Chad and Zeke had been dreading this test since their freshman year, because most colleges used SAT scores to determine which students would be admitted and, more to the point, which would be rejected. Zeke and Chad earned good grades, but the idea of sitting in a room for three hours and taking a test that would decide what colleges they would or would not get into . . . well, that was more pressure than shooting a free throw in the last five seconds of a basketball game!

There was no way you could call anything to do with the SATs 'fun', Zeke thought. This was just further evidence to support his pet theory that Principal Matsui was actually from a different planet. Possibly a different universe.

"Be sure to sign up in the office as soon as possible, because these sessions are filling up fast!" the principal went on.

Sharpay rolled her eyes. He was starting to sound like one of those desperate salespeople on late-night TV commercials, she thought, the ones who tried to persuade you to buy hair de-frizzers and sardine-filleting knives.

"So, sign up!" he repeated. "Now!"

There was a long moment of silence as the principal apparently paused for dramatic effect. Gabriella glanced around the room. No one seemed very psyched about the SAT tutoring sessions.

She sighed. She didn't really want to be a brainiac, but it was in her nature. She couldn't help it – she *did* think that trying to get a high

5

SAT score would be kind of fun. It was a contest, just like trying to win a basketball game or get the lead in a school play – and no one thought *those* competitions were boring . . .

Her thoughts were interrupted by Principal Matsui, who had finally reached the last announcement of the day.

"And now, I have one final and very exciting bit of news!" His voice boomed from the PA speaker. "The Student Council has decided on the theme for this year's Halloween Festival, and I think it's one that every student will enjoy. The theme is 'Future Fantasy'. Everyone is invited to come to the festival dressed as the person they think they'll be in twenty years. Here's a chance to have fun, be creative – oh, and give a little thought to what your future is going to be! So get started on those costumes, and I look forward to seeing a glimpse into the future in a couple of weeks!"

That woke everyone up. An excited buzz broke out in the classroom.

"This is awesome, Sharpay!" Ryan cried, his

eyes sparkling. "Just think of all the possibilities! You could be a singer, or an actress, or a Broadway dancer–"

"Yes," Sharpay said softly, looking into the distance as if she could see her future unfolding before her. "I could be anything. But the one thing I will be is – a *star*!"

"You mean you're going to dress as a massive body of plasma in outer space, which is held together by its own gravity?" Chad asked innocently.

Sharpay glared at him. "I wouldn't expect someone like *you* to understand," she sniffed. "What are you going to dress as – a has-been basketball player?"

"My skills on the court will be duly covered in my VH-1 special," Chad said, unruffled by her snide tone. "That is, once I make a billion dollars and become a huge hip-hop star! In fact, I gotta go out and buy some bling this weekend. Can't walk into the Halloween party looking like I got no game."

"That's right." Zeke reached over to give him

a high five. "And I've gotta get one of those white chef's jackets."

"And the hat," Chad said. "One of those tall white hats with the puffy top."

"A toque," Zeke said.

"Uh . . . what?" Chad replied, puzzled.

"That's what a chef's hat is called," Zeke explained patiently. "I learned that in French class." He brightened and added enthusiastically, "I'm really glad I decided to take French because it is a great language for bakers! Like, I just found out that I've been pronouncing crème brûlée wrong for years, and that there's a French cookie called a madeleine that sounds really awesome, and—"

The bell rang, interrupting Zeke, and Chad breathed a sigh of relief. When Zeke started talking about baking, he could go on for hours.

Chad and Zeke hurriedly said goodbye and headed to their next class, leaving Troy and Gabriella alone together.

"Maybe a bunch of us could go shopping for

costumes after school. What kind of costume are you going to wear?" Gabriella asked.

Troy grinned at her. "I think it'll be more fun if I make you guess."

"Ohhh," she said, smiling back. "It's a deep, dark secret, huh? Well, I know I'll be able to figure it out when I see what you buy."

"Don't be so sure. But here's a hint: I've had my costume picked out for years." He winked at her and walked down the hall.

Gabriella looked after him, still smiling, but now quite curious as well.

Hordes of students were rushing through the halls, trying to get to their next class before the late bell rang. Gabriella clutched her books tightly as she was jostled by the crowd. There was a sudden surge to the left and Sharpay brushed past her, catching her off guard just as she was walking past the principal's office. She stumbled and almost fell, but Principal Matsui reached out a hand to catch her.

"Oh, thanks," Gabriella said.

"I'm glad to see that you're so eager to start learning today, Sharpay," he said. "Better slow down, though. We don't want any unfortunate accidents – especially any involving our star tutor for the SATs!"

Sharpay's forehead creased in a tiny frown. "What do you mean?" she asked, before remembering that frowning caused wrinkles. She quickly smoothed out her expression and stared blandly at Principal Matsui. "Are you talking about Gabriella?"

"Indeed I am!" the principal beamed. He smiled fondly at Gabriella. "She's in charge of the entire SAT tutoring programme!"

Gabriella blushed. "It's not that big a deal–"

"No, no, I'm very excited about the new method you suggested," Principal Matsui insisted. "Having our students help each other study for the test could potentially take us to a whole new level! I anticipate East High students earning SAT scores that are more than respectable! In fact, I predict–" He paused to take a deep breath, then continued dramatically, "–I confidently predict that this year's class will beat the record set back in 1976 for the school's highest SAT scores ever!"

Sharpay rolled her eyes. "Whatever."

Principal Matsui frowned. He hated it when students rolled their eyes. And he *really* hated it when they said "whatever" in that bored voice.

"It might be a good idea for you to look beyond the horizon of the drama department, Sharpay," the principal said sternly. "In fact–"

Gabriella started shaking her head, praying that she could get him to stop in midsentence. She knew what was coming next.

And, just as she guessed, the principal continued, "–you should take a page from Gabriella here. Now *she* believes in hitting the books. *She* takes her education seriously."

Sharpay delicately raised one eyebrow. Gabriella had to admire her acting skills. With one simple facial movement, she managed to convey a world of scorn. "Hmm," she purred. "That is a good attitude, I suppose—"

The principal nodded, satisfied that he had made his point.

Sharpay added, "—although it does make a person sound like a bit of a drudge, don't you think?"

Gabriella flinched.

"Well, drudge is a harsh word," Mr Matsui said mildly. "I'd suggest something more along the lines of 'ambitious' or 'hardworking'."

Sharpay rolled her eyes again. "Whatever."

Mr Matsui silently counted to ten and said, "You might consider signing up for the tutoring sessions yourself, Sharpay. Even a future star may want to go to college and have something to fall back on. Who knows, you might end up with a career in – er—" He stopped, clearly unable to think of any profession that would be appropriate for her.

"TV news?" Gabriella suggested. Mr Matsui

shot her a grateful look as she went on. "Maybe you could be a reporter on one of those entertainment shows?"

Sharpay stared at both of them, completely speechless. *Something to fall back on? An entertainment reporter?* The idea of reporting on *other* people's success . . . the mere thought made her physically ill.

"Please!" Sharpay said. "I will be the one on the red carpet being interviewed, *not* the person asking inane questions!"

Principal Matsui couldn't help himself. He rolled his eyes. "Whatever," he snapped, then he stomped down the hall.

"Sorry about that." Gabriella smiled apologetically at Sharpay. "Mr Matsui gets a little intense when it comes to standardized tests."

"That's all right." Sharpay tossed her hair in a manner that she knew (from many nights of practice in front of the mirror) was quite becoming. Sure enough, a few boys glanced her way. One of them walked into an open locker door.

Sharpay's smile widened. "I'm used to having my talent misunderstood."

Then she glanced meaningfully at Gabriella's armful of books and added sweetly, "But those tutoring sessions sound just perfect for *you*. Have fun!"

Then Sharpay gave a little wave and sauntered down the hall, leaving Gabriella feeling like the dictionary definition of *drudge*.

CHAPTER TWO

"Take a look at this hat, Troy," Taylor McKessie said. She pulled a grey fedora from a shelf in the second-hand shop and handed it to him. He put it on, pulling the brim down over his eyes. "Cool! You look just like an international spy!"

He grinned, but he took the hat off and put it back. "That's one career that is definitely not in my future. I'm terrible at keeping secrets."

"You've been doing a good job of keeping your costume a secret," Gabriella teased him.

"That's because I know it's driving you crazy!" Troy said, laughing.

Gabriella playfully turned to Chad. "Chad, do you know how Troy's going to dress for the party?"

"Nope." Chad began pawing through a basket filled with costume jewellery. "And even if I did, I couldn't tell. Troy's my boy. My lips are sealed!"

"We'll find out soon enough," Taylor said, sighing. "In the meantime, Gabriella, what are you doing with that hideous dress?"

Gabriella held a grey dress up in front of her. The hem fell three inches below her knees. The lace collar looked dingy and worn. She frowned at her reflection in the mirror. "I don't know," she admitted. "I started thinking that maybe I'll be a college science professor . . . does this look right?"

"Hmmm . . . I think you can do better," Taylor said firmly. "Keep looking!"

As Gabriella hung up the dress, Taylor reached past her to pull a skirt and jacket off the rack. "Now these, on the other hand, have definite possibilities," she said.

Chad's eyes widened in disbelief. "Are you crazy?" he asked. "That looks like one of the suits my mum wears to work."

"Exactly." Taylor nodded smugly.

Troy, Gabriella and Chad exchanged confused glances.

"Um, Taylor? I thought you said you wanted a costume that was really cool," Troy said. "Don't get mad, but that looks kind of, well . . . dull."

"It just needs a few alterations," Taylor said, holding the suit away from her so that she could get a better look. "I'll definitely take the hem up a few inches. And the jacket needs to be a little more formfitting. But with superhigh heels, sheer stockings, a silk blouse, and the right earrings – yep, I can definitely make this work." She grinned at her friends. "Can you guess what I'm going as?"

Chad squinted his eyes as if that would help

him guess. After a moment, he sighed and shook his head. "I don't have a clue. Maybe something in business?"

"Not even close," Taylor said smugly.

"A bank president?" Troy suggested.

"Nice try." Taylor laughed. "But think bigger."

"A lawyer?" Gabriella guessed. That was what Chad's mother did for a living and she was very smart and very successful. Still, it did seem like a rather ordinary ambition for someone like Taylor. Over the past year, she had learned that her friend didn't just dream big dreams – she dreamed *enormous* dreams.

"Bigger . . ." Taylor teased.

After a long moment, her friends all shook their heads.

"We give up," Troy said. "Come on, let us in on the secret."

"All right. I am going to be dressed as–" Taylor paused dramatically, enjoying the moment of suspense. "–the first woman president of the United States!"

As soon as she said that, the others laughed. Of course! It was so *obvious*.

"I should have known that your address would eventually be the White House," Gabriella said.

"You've got my vote," Troy agreed.

But Chad looked dubious. "I don't know if that fits your image, Taylor. I mean, presidents always look so boring."

"I know. But that is just the first thing I plan to change," she answered loftily. "I am going to be the first president with *style*."

An hour later, Taylor had found the perfect pointy-toed, high-heeled shoes to complete her outfit. Chad was standing in front of a full-length mirror, admiring his reflection. He had looped several gold necklaces around his neck. Even though the necklaces were just costume jewellery, and rather tarnished costume jewellery at that, the effect was good. He was especially proud of the necklace that had a large gold dollar sign hanging from it.

"What do you guys think?" he asked.

"Awesome," Troy said. "Now if you could only rhyme—"

"Hey, don't go disparaging my hip-hop abilities, man!" Chad grinned.

"I'm not disparaging them, I'm doubting they even exist," Troy teased.

"Wait until you see me on MTV," Chad said, pretending to be annoyed. "Then you'll be begging to roll with me and my crew."

Gabriella smiled. "But really, Chad, what kind of career do you think you'd like? I mean, it's fun to pretend, but isn't the costume supposed to be based on what you're really planning to do with your life?"

Chad turned back to the mirror. "Well, it kind of is," he murmured, not looking at any of them.

"Really?" Taylor realized, a second too late, that she sounded far too amazed. "You want to be a hip-hop star?"

Chad shuffled his feet and gave a tiny shrug. "Not exactly. I mean, I know I can't really perform the way those guys do. But I love the music, and I know everything about it. I read all the magazines and blogs that are out there, and I have just about every hip-hop CD ever made. I guess I wish I could do something with it, you know—"

"But you can," Gabriella said, excited. "You could work at a music company, finding new artists. Or you could design the CD covers or write the songs or work in publicity. There are all kinds of jobs in the music business."

Chad looked at her, surprised. "Hey, I never thought of that."

"That's a great idea," Troy said. "Nobody knows more about music than you."

"Well, maybe not at East High," Chad agreed modestly.

He looked at Troy, who was flipping through a stack of old record albums. "Hey, dude, you still haven't told us what your costume's going to be."

"Yeah," Gabriella said. "And you still haven't tried anything on."

"I don't need to," Troy said. "I've known what I want to do forever."

"What's that?" she asked.

He shrugged. "Go to the University of Arizona, play basketball, and maybe–" He knocked wood. "–even go pro. And after that, get a job as a coach or maybe a sportswriter."

"I should have known!" Chad said. He turned to Gabriella. "Troy's been talking about that since he was eight years old."

"Yep." Troy sat down in an ancient plaid recliner, stretched out and put his hands behind his head. "I figure I'll just wear my basketball uniform. No fuss, no muss, no money spent on fancy costumes."

Chad shook his head in admiration. "Must be sweet, having everything all figured out."

"Yep." Troy smiled smugly.

"Well, I guess I'm not going to find anything here," Gabriella sighed, as she began hanging up the pile of clothes that were lying on a nearby table. For the past hour, she had pulled one item after another off the rack, only to have them all soundly rejected by Taylor.

"Yeah, those are pretty sad," Troy agreed. He picked up a brown polyester trouser suit and held it at arm's length, as if it might contaminate him. "The 70s were seriously weird when it came to clothes," he commented.

"Hey, I have an idea!" Chad said brightly. "Don't go as a science professor – go as a mad scientist! You could wear those crazy goggle eyeglasses and frizz your hair out and even dye it green! Man, you would look awesome!"

Gabriella and Taylor looked at each other and rolled their eyes.

"Chad, she is going to a party!" Taylor said.

He looked puzzled. "Yeah, so?"

"So she wants to look cute, not crazy!" Taylor cried.

"What's wrong with looking crazy?" Chad asked. "You know what would make that costume even better? Some of those fake teeth, the gnarly, crooked ones with fungus on them–"

"That is disgusting!" Taylor groaned.

"Thanks for the suggestions, Chad, but I think I'll pass," Gabriella said, trying her best to smile. She knew Chad was just joking around, but his teasing had made a sudden wave of doubt sweep over her. She was going to be the worst-dressed person at the party! Everyone else was going to look great, and she was going to look like a troll who lived in a library! Why did the Student Council have to come up with this weird theme anyway. . . ?

Troy caught Gabriella's eye and gave her a little wink. "You'll look great, no matter what you wear," he said softly. "You always do."

She smiled, feeling a little glow inside at his reassuring words. Taylor was right; the Halloween party should be fun. All she had to do was come up with a good costume — how hard could that be?

CHAPTER THREE

The next afternoon, a dozen East High students gathered in Room 127B after the last bell rang. Most of them sat slumped in their chairs, looking bored, irritated or, at best, unenthusiastic. Several looked wistfully out of the window at the warm, bright afternoon they were missing. And a few already had their heads down on their desks. Gabriella stood at the front of the class, surveyed the members of her first SAT tutoring session and gulped.

She quickly glanced at the other peer tutors she had recruited – Taylor, of course, plus Jenny from honours French and Danny from advanced calculus – who were huddled together in the back of the room. They looked worried. Gabriella didn't blame them. The room was filled with the gloomy air of anxiety and defeat.

"Okay!" she said brightly, "I'm so glad to see such a great turnout! Thanks for coming, every-one!" Even to her own ears, she sounded as fake and bright as an aluminium Christmas tree.

A dozen pairs of eyes stared at her blankly. Gabriella felt her palms getting sweaty. This was even worse than singing onstage in front of hundreds of people!

Then she noticed Chad sitting in the back row. He gave her a big smile and a thumbs-up, and she relaxed a little bit. At least there's one friendly face here, she thought.

She smiled back at him and started again. "So! Why don't we get started by, um . . ." She glanced down at the clipboard she had been clutching since she walked into the room. It held the sign-up sheet for the tutoring session. "Oh, yes! Why don't we get started by signing the sign-up sheet. . . ?"

Gabriella handed the clipboard to Alicia, one of Sharpay's Drama-Club friends who had been a member of Sharpay and the Sharpettes in the school's Battle of the Bands.

"And while that's going around, why don't we each say why we decided to sign up for SAT tutoring," Gabriella continued. She paused. Dead silence greeted this idea. "Um . . . anybody?"

After the longest fifteen seconds in Gabriella's life, Alicia finally raised her hand.

"Yes!" Gabriella pointed to her.

"I signed up for peer tutoring because my parents said I had to," Alicia said cheerfully. "They said getting a *real* tutor would cost too much money."

"Oh. Well. Thanks for sharing," Gabriella said. "Now, anyone else?" She pointed to a short boy with wild, wavy, brown hair and an intense expression. "What's your name?"

"Nathan James." He sounded tense and he blinked rapidly a few times, as if unnerved by being called upon.

"Hi, Nathan." Gabriella tried to sound soothing. "So, why are you—"

"Because I need an edge!" Nathan broke in before Gabriella could finish her sentence. "I need every edge I can get! I've already got *The Official SAT Study Guide, The SAT Question-a-Day Calendar* and every single one of the SAT practice test downloads, but it still may not be enough! And I *have* to get a better score this time around!"

Gabriella raised her eyebrows in surprise. "This time?"

He nodded impatiently, as if he shouldn't have to explain this. "I've already taken the test twice! My last two scores were 2290 and 2340 and I know that if I work hard enough I can get a 2400!" His eyes glittered. "A perfect score!

That's my goal! That's my ambition! That's my reason for being here!"

There was a short silence.

Then Chad muttered, "Dude, chill out. It's only a test."

There were a few snickers. Nathan whirled around. "Only a test?" he cried. *"Only . . . a . . . test?* The margin between success and failure in life is razor thin, and the SATs are the first clear indicator of what our futures will be!" He shook his head in disbelief and muttered, "Only a test!" once more before opening a study guide and immersing himself in its pages.

Gabriella could feel the tension in the room rise again. "Well, that may be a little bit of an overstatement," she began.

But, at that moment, the classroom door flew open as if pushed by a strong wind. Every head in the room turned to see Sharpay standing in the doorway, striking a haughty pose. "Am I in the right place?" she demanded. Her gaze swept the room. She curled her lip in disdain. "Hmm . . .

the atmosphere seems suitably dull and drab, so I guess this must be the SAT tutoring class."

"For your information, we are here to work," Taylor snapped. "If you want excitement, why don't you go find a spotlight somewhere?"

"Love to," Sharpay snapped back. "But–"

"–we're being *forced* to get tutoring!" Ryan said, peeking over her shoulder. He turned to Gabriella and whispered, "I'm sorry, I know you helped me so much when you tutored me in algebra. But coming here, to be tutored with an entire group of people?!" He shuddered, and his voice began to rise as he continued. "It's like being assigned to a chain gang! Or being forced to work eighteen hours a day in a factory! Or being apprenticed to an evil master because there isn't enough food for all the kids in the family!"

He paused for breath.

"Been reading a lot of Charles Dickens lately?" Taylor murmured.

He gave her a puzzled look. "What?"

She sighed and shook her head. "Never mind."

"Listen, I don't want anyone here if they don't want to be–" Gabriella began.

"Then neither one of us is getting what she wants, is she?" Sharpay's mind flashed back to the evening before, and the very dramatic – one might even say *heart-wrenching* – performance she had delivered at the dining-room table. But her parents had refused to accept that she was destined to become a superstar through sheer genius and insisted that she try to get into a good college instead. "Never mind. I shall make the best of a bad situation, as always."

She walked to a desk near the window, her head held high, her chin firm with resolve, and her eyes shining with the hint of tears – the very picture of a brave, yet doomed, victim.

Ryan watched her, his face shining with admiration. "That's a perfect attitude for when you play Joan of Arc," he said. "Remember this moment, Sharpay!"

"It is seared into my memory," she replied throatily, as she sat down with exquisite poise and grace.

Taylor rolled her eyes. "And the Oscar goes to . . ."

Twenty minutes later, they had divided into small groups led by Taylor, Jenny and Danny, the student tutors. The students at Taylor's table were listening intently as she explained how they would study for the test over the coming weeks. Jenny was calming everyone's nerves by telling them, in detail, how the test was formatted. And Danny, it turned out, had an unsuspected affinity for gallows humour. He already had everyone at his table laughing at the thought of taking on the SAT math section.

At Gabriella's table, however, things were not going so well.

As soon as everyone had started to divide into groups, Sharpay had pushed her way over to Gabriella, with Ryan at her side, as always. "I want to be in your group!" she said. "In fact, I must be in your group! I insist on it!"

"Really?" Gabriella couldn't hide the surprise in her voice. "Um . . . why?"

Sharpay tossed her hair haughtily. "I heard what Principal Matsui said about you in the hall. He said you were the *star* tutor!"

"Of course, that is a gross misuse of the word 'star'," Ryan said, "but Ms Darbus always says that high school principals know *nothing* about showbiz."

Sharpay gave him a frosty look at this interruption.

"Sorry," he murmured, staring at the floor.

"*Anyway,*" Sharpay went on. "The point is, that means you are the best at what you do – just like me. So, if I must be here, I deserve to have the best tutor possible."

"It's just like Ms Darbus always says," Ryan interrupted again. "A true star surrounds herself with the best cast and crew so that she will look as *awesome* as possible!"

"O-kay," Gabriella said slowly. "I'll be happy to help you and Ryan and–" She turned to see the other members of the group. Gabriella smiled as Chad pulled out a chair at her table, but her heart sank a little to see that Nathan had also seated himself there, his right foot jiggling with impatience. "–Chad and Nathan. First, let's get to know a little bit about each other–"

"Waste of time," Nathan interrupted. "Every minute we spend chatting is one less minute spent preparing!"

Before Gabriella could answer, the door opened again and Principal Matsui entered the room.

"Good afternoon, everyone!" he said, as he walked to the front of the classroom. "I'm certainly glad to see you all here, getting ready to *rock the SATs!*"

Utter silence greeted this remark. Mr Matsui cleared his throat and went on more calmly. "Now, I know that some of you might be a little worried right now. Maybe you're frightened by the thought of sitting in a room for a couple of hours, answering hundreds of questions designed to test everything you've learned in twelve years of school. Maybe you're intimidated by the thought of your score determining what college you get into, which could, in turn, affect the course of your entire life!"

Gabriella gulped. This wasn't exactly going to calm everyone's nerves, she thought. As if Mr Matsui had read her mind, he quickly changed course.

"But I have every confidence in you!" he beamed. "East High students are the best in the state! I know that you are all going to work very hard so that you can do the best possible job when you finally take the test. And remember – we're trying to beat the school's all-time record for highest SAT scores, a record that has gone unchallenged for more than thirty years. So . . . best of luck to all of you!"

He gave them a thumbs-up and another cheerful wave as he left the room.

Gabriella glanced around at everyone. Chad was frowning with worry. Nathan was biting his lip. Ryan moaned quietly to himself. Even Sharpay looked a little pale.

"Don't worry," she said quickly. "Remember, if you're prepared, you won't be scared. And that preparation starts now."

CHAPTER FOUR

"Class, I must tell you that I have been completely inspired by the theme for this year's Halloween party!" It was the next day, and Ms Darbus stood in front of the classroom, her eyes shining with enthusiasm. "After all, isn't theatre all about looking into the future and imaginatively exploring the many, many possibilities open to us?"

"I thought it was about exploring all the many possible ways to mess up your lines," Chad muttered to Zeke, who stifled a laugh. During their freshman year, Chad had once had a small part with only five lines, all of which he had managed to forget on the night of the performance. He had also tripped three times while onstage and accidentally knocked over a small table. That was the night he had vowed to become a permanent member of the stage crew.

Ms Darbus glared at Zeke, who bit his lip and settled back in his chair.

"That is why today we are going to do an exercise in active visualization," she went on. "Now, I want you all to imagine that you are about to turn a hundred. In honour of this occasion, a newspaper reporter has come to your house to interview you—"

"Hey, if I live to be a hundred, that reporter better be ready to rock out, 'cause I'm going to be having a party!" Chad interrupted.

"That's enough, Mr Danforth," Ms Darbus sniffed. "Now, as I was saying . . . to do this exercise, I want you to pair off and take turns playing the reporter. If you are the one being interviewed, you need to talk about everything you've done in your century of life, decade by decade. Are we clear?"

Chad opened his mouth as if to answer but was quelled by Ms Darbus's glare.

"Yes," he said meekly.

"Good. Now, I want you to really feel the moment when you're playing the part of someone who is a hundred years old. Inhabit the role. And let your imaginations run wild!"

Troy moved over to sit next to Chad. He shook his head in disapproval at his friend, even though he couldn't help smiling. "Man, haven't you had enough detention from Darbus?"

Chad grinned. "I know, I know. But you know class clowns always end up as wealthy and beloved comedians when they grow up! I figure I'm just laying the groundwork here."

"So, let's get started," Troy said. "Tell me, Mr Danforth, what are your favourite memories from your long and illustrious life?"

"Well, I'd have to start with winning the Grammy for producing a million-selling hip-hop album when I was only twenty-four," Chad began breezily. "Then, as the whole world knows, I became an actor. I'd have to say that winning an Oscar for my very first movie was also a highlight. . . ."

Fifteen minutes later, Troy was taking his turn being "interviewed" about his life. Compared to Chad, it was pretty slow going.

"So then I graduated from college," he was saying as Ms Darbus walked over to them. "And then I, um, got a job at *ESPN The Magazine* writing about basketball. . . ."

He stopped, his mind blank as he tried to think of something else to say. It was a little unnerving to realize that he had no idea what would come next; it was even more unnerving to have the drama teacher staring at him, her mouth pursed as she listened.

"And then I, uh, decided to write about foot-ball, too," he continued, wildly searching for something else to say. "And then, um . . ."

His voice trailed off.

"Your imagination seems to be stuck in low gear, Troy," Ms Darbus commented. "Can't you think of something to do with your life that doesn't involve . . ." She curled her lip in disdain. " . . . *sports*?"

"Sure," Troy said. "Let's see . . . after *ESPN The Magazine*, I became a, uh—"

"Veterinarian!" Chad jumped in to rescue his buddy. "Remember how you used to beg your mom to get you a dog?"

Somehow, Troy didn't think that asking for a puppy for Christmas when he was five really meant much in terms of future career choices . . . but he'd say anything to make Ms Darbus move on. "Yeah, that's right! So, let's see, after college, I went to vet school, then I opened my own office, and then . . ."

"That's better," Ms Darbus commented. "You see? It's all about *embracing* the possibilities!"

As she wandered off to another pair of

students, Chad gave Troy a "we got out of another tight spot" wink, but Troy kept talking, just to make sure that Ms Darbus didn't circle back and put him on the spot again.

"I specialized in, um, large animals," he went on, thinking vaguely of large dogs or small ponies. Then he came up with something even more interesting. "In fact, the bigger and more dangerous they were, the better! I became known throughout the state as the person to call when you found an alligator in your swimming pool or a python in your pine tree!"

"Alligators? Pythons?" Chad interrupted. "Where are you living, oh future Troy, in some kind of tropical paradise?"

"Hey, that's not a bad idea," Troy said, brightening at the thought of warm sun and tropical sand. After all, if he was supposed to use his imagination, why not imagine settling down on a nice beach, maybe in the Caribbean . . . ? "So, I became known and revered throughout the Caribbean for my almost mystical ability to soothe savage beasts. But after a few years, I got bored with fending off deadly vipers, so I decided to try something new. . . "

Once he got started, Troy found that the exercise was actually pretty easy. Even more surprisingly, he discovered that it was a lot of fun. He had always been so sure of what his future held that he had never spent much time thinking about it. Now, as he talked on and on to an increasingly bored Chad, he seemed to be able to visualize more alternative lives than he could count.

"And then I used my knowledge about animals to get a television show!" he said. "I started travelling around the world, filming animals in their natural habitats! I published several best-selling books about my work, and then—"

The bell rang to end class. Chad wearily lifted his head from his desk, where he had been pretending to snore.

"And then your best friend was finally released into the wild, free to roam the halls of his high school without listening to page two hundred of your autobiography," he said.

"Okay, maybe I got a little carried away," Troy grinned. "But once I got started, it was like I was watching a movie on TV! All I had to do was talk about what I was seeing on the screen."

"A movie? Dude, that was more like a mini-series!" Chad said. "You'd better surf on back to the sports channel before you ditch basketball for biology class – permanently!"

"Okay, let's go over this question again," Gabriella said wearily later that afternoon at the tutoring session. She rubbed the spot just above her nose, where a throbbing headache was beginning to develop. "There are twenty-five players on the first string of the high school football team. There are twenty players on the second string. And there are twenty players on the third string. Now, the coach – yes, Ryan?"

"Football?" Ryan's forehead was creased with

worry. "I didn't know we were going to be tested on football! That doesn't seem fair! Isn't it enough that we have to learn math? And English? And *science*?"

"This isn't really a question about football—" Gabriella began.

"But you said there were three strings of football players!" Ryan sounded as if he were about to hyperventilate. "I don't even know what those are!"

"Oh, oh, oh, I do! I know this!" Sharpay's hand was waving in the air. "Remember when I was dating Pete Campbell?"

"Of course! The captain of the East High Wildcats!" Ryan's panic receded slightly at the thought that Sharpay was on top of this. "You were like the supercouple of East High!"

"I know. I thought that the editor of the school paper might come up with a cute name for us, like Shar-pete." She rolled her eyes in exasperation. "But she had the nerve to say that she was a journalist, not a gossip columnist.

Honestly! No wonder people don't trust the press anymore!"

"Focus, people! Work the problem!" Nathan snapped. "If you keep getting sidetracked like this during the test, you are going to be *road kill*!"

Ryan's eyes widened with terror. Chad began nervously shredding a piece of notebook paper.

"Um, well, that might be putting it a little strongly," Gabriella said hastily.

"Really?" Nathan sneered. "And how many times have *you* taken the SATs?"

Gabriella blushed. "I haven't taken them yet," she admitted. "But I know we'll all do better if we can remain calm and positive–"

Nathan gave a little snort. "Positive thinking is for people who aren't prepared. And that is not me." He reached into his book bag and pulled out a flat cardboard box. "Look at what I just bought!"

Ryan leaned over and tried to read what was written on the top of the box. He was reading upside down, which made the task even harder. "The . . . SAT . . . um . . ."

"The Official SAT Board Game!" Nathan snapped. He opened the box and pulled out a game board which was covered with colourful squares and boxes. "Take a look at this. See, you roll the dice and move your marker the correct number of spaces. . . ." He pointed to the proper space. "So, I landed on that square, which has the number eighty-seven on it. That means I find question number eighty-seven in this book. . . ." He pulled a thick manual from the box. "Then I answer it, check the answer, and, if it's right, I get to move forward three spaces."

"Oooh, that sounds even more fun than Candyland!" Chad said, his voice dripping with sarcasm.

"It's not supposed to be fun!" Nathan said impatiently. "It's supposed to prepare you for the test by simulating the random nature of the questions you'll be asked."

"Is that really necessary?" Gabriella asked,

trying not to sound too dubious. "I mean, studying for a couple of hours a night might be just as effective. . . ."

But Nathan was confidently reading quotes from the back of the box. "'This product raised my scores by 27 percent!' says Jan T. from Wilsbury, Maine. 'I wouldn't have been accepted to Harvard without the Official SAT Board Game!' says Mike B. from Juniper, Oregon. 'You saved my academic life!' says–"

"Sounds like a great product. But let's go back to the question we were working on," Gabriella interrupted. "Sharpay, you were saying–"

"Oh, yes!" Sharpay brightened up again. "So the second-string players are like the understudies to the first string. They play when the really good players are tired or something. And the third string players are like the understudies for the understudies, which means they hardly ever get to play–"

"I think we all understand the concept of under – I mean, of first, second and third-string players," Gabriella said. "But that really has nothing to do with this problem. As I was about to say, the football team is travelling to an away game, and the coach can only take forty players. How many will the coach have to leave at home?"

Ryan and Chad stared at her blankly as Sharpay turned her attention to her fingernails, admiring her new manicure.

"Come on, this is easy," Gabriella said, an encouraging note in her voice.

Ryan's eyes got even wider with fear, and he began breathing rapidly.

Recognizing the signs of rising panic, Gabriella calmly suggested, "Do you want to look over your notes?"

Ryan flipped back a few pages in his notebook. One page, Gabriella noticed, had a detailed drawing of a costume for *The Phantom of the Opera*, while another had a sketch of a very spooky set design. None of the pages seemed to have any notes about percentages or, for that matter, anything else to do with SATs.

"This isn't helping!" he cried, a rising note of panic in his voice. Sweat broke out on his forehead. "Nothing is helping!"

Sharpay gave an irritated sigh. "The answer is twenty-five," she said sharply.

Gabriella raised her eyebrows in surprise. She didn't think Sharpay had even been paying attention, let alone figuring out the answer. . .

"Thank you!" Ryan said to his sister. His tone was as heartfelt as if she had just pulled him from the path of a speeding train. "I don't know what I'd do without you!"

"Hey, man, she's not going to be able to give you the answers when we're taking the test," Chad said. "And the SATs are only three weeks away. That's only, like, twenty-one days!"

Ryan turned pale. "We're doomed! Completely and totally doomed!"

Gabriella sighed, rubbed her forehead again and tried to think of something positive to say. Unfortunately, her mind was blank. Even worse, she was beginning to agree with Ryan.

CHAPTER FIVE

The next day after school, Gabriella went to the gym to meet Troy. Even though the SAT tutoring sessions had been her idea, she was secretly relieved to have an afternoon off to just hang out. As she walked through the gym doors, she saw that basketball practice had just ended. The players gathered in a circle around Coach Bolton at the side of the court.

"Great job, guys," the coach said. "Everybody showed good hustle on the suicide drills and that new pass-and-weave play is really looking sharp. I think we're in good shape for next week's game. You know what to do – you just have to keep your focus on that." He put his hand out in the middle of the circle. The players all put their hands out as well and then yelled, "Go Wildcats!" throwing their hands into the air.

As the team headed for the locker room, Coach Bolton stopped Troy. "Hold on a sec, will you?"

"Sure. What's going on?"

"I got a phone call this morning," the coach said. "A scouting agent from the University of Arizona is coming to our first game."

Troy nodded. This was nothing new. The East High basketball team was one of the best in the state. Scouts came from universities all over the country to see them play. "Okay," he said easily. "We'll put on a good show."

Coach Bolton smiled slightly. "I'd expect nothing less from you guys, whether there was a scout in the audience or not. But here's the thing

– I heard through the grapevine that the player this guy is most interested in looking at is . . . you."

"Really?"

"Yeah. I almost didn't tell you . . . I didn't want you to be distracted from your game. But here's where I quit being your coach and start being your dad." Troy's father smiled a little sheepishly. "I don't want to put pressure on you, but I think you could get a basketball scholarship. I know you're good enough."

"Thanks," Troy said automatically, but, for once, his dad's praise didn't warm him up inside. In fact, he felt a slight flutter of nerves in his stomach.

What's wrong with me? he wondered. This is just another game. And having a college scout here to watch me . . . I've waited my whole life for this chance!

His dad patted him on the shoulder. "Okay. Enough said. Why don't you hit the showers and–" He turned to see Gabriella standing by the bleachers and smiled. "–go out for a pizza or something? Relax. Don't even think about the game, all right?"

"Sure," Troy said, even though he knew he'd be thinking of nothing else.

Gabriella took one last bite of pizza and dropped the crust onto her plate. "That was awesome," she said. "Pepperoni and pineapple. Two things that shouldn't work together, but somehow–"

"–they just do." Troy finished her sentence happily, taking another huge bite. Until he'd met Gabriella, Troy had never known another person who liked pepperoni and pineapple pizza. Now it was their favourite meal. They ordered it when-ever they were able to hang out together, just by themselves.

Gabriella smiled back at him and sipped her drink.

They had talked about the SAT tutoring sessions (and agreed that they couldn't wait to take the test so that they could quit thinking about it).

They had gone over the paper their history teacher had just assigned (and decided that they should go to the library together on Saturday to get a head start on their research). And they had discussed, in great detail, the latest playlists they had created on their MP3 players and why they were better than every other playlist in the entire history of recorded music.

But even though Gabriella felt relaxed and easy talking with Troy, she sensed that he was a little preoccupied. She decided to casually mention what she had overheard his father say to him at the end of practice.

"So, are you nervous about having a scout at the game?" she asked.

"Not too much," he said.

"Uh-huh," she answered.

He heard the scepticism in her voice and grinned. "Well, yeah, a little. I guess I've got a few butterflies in my stomach. I mean, I can barely eat."

She laughed out loud.

"What?" he asked, faintly offended.

She pointed to his plate, which contained nothing but a few pieces of crust. "You seemed to have managed three slices of pizza pretty well," she teased.

"Busted!" He grinned. "Okay, not much is going to get in the way of a slice of pepperoni and pineapple pizza. But, seriously . . . I kind of wish my dad hadn't told me about the scout."

"You guys have been working really hard," Gabriella said. "I'm sure you'll do great."

"Yeah . . ." He paused, then said, "Actually, I don't think I'm really nervous about playing well. It's more the idea of college. . . ." His voice trailed off, then he shrugged and gave her a sheepish grin. "Now that I'm a senior, the future seems a lot closer than it used to."

"I know what you mean," she said. "But we've still got plenty of time to figure everything out."

Troy nodded, "I guess you're right."

"And speaking of figuring things out . . ." she began.

He raised one eyebrow. "Yes?"

"Are you still going to wear your basketball uniform to the party?" she asked. "Because I've been having a hard time figuring out my costume, and it's really starting to bug me–"

But Troy wasn't listening. "I'm not sure about that costume anymore," he said, frowning. His voice trailed off as a picture flashed into his mind. He was speeding down a snowy mountain under a bright blue sky, perfectly balanced on his skis, enjoying the feeling of cold wind on his face. . . .

Gabriella took another sip of her drink. "I thought you were totally set on a career in sports," she said.

"Yeah," he said slowly. "I was. But here's the thing . . ." He leaned forward and went on more eagerly. "I was thinking about that holiday resort where you and I first met, remember?"

Gabriella smiled. "Of course."

She waited for Troy to say something, well, maybe a little romantic about the night they first sang together in a karaoke contest.

Instead, he went on, "I took some snowboard lessons that week. The instructor was a really cool guy who taught skiing and snowboarding all winter, then worked as a whitewater-rafting guide all summer. That would be a great way to make a living, don't you think?" He leaned back in his chair and gave a huge sigh. "But I don't know, maybe that's crazy. Maybe I should really hit the books and get a high-paying job at some corporation! But people always say you should focus on what you like, and I love basketball!"

He stopped to take a breath. "So, what do you think I should do, Gabriella?"

She opened her mouth to reply, then shut it again, feeling totally confused. How had they gone from eating pizza to talking about careers? And how could she help Troy when she was so totally preoccupied with thinking about her own costume and her own future?

She pushed her drink back and started gathering her books. "I don't know, Troy," she said. Trying to lighten the mood, she added, "Maybe you should have made an appointment with the careers counsellor instead of going out with me this afternoon."

But he completely missed the joke. In fact, his eyes lit up at her suggestion. "Great idea!" he said. "I think I'll swing by her office tomorrow!" He took one last bite of pizza and gazed earnestly at her. "What kind of stuff do you think I should ask her?"

Gabriella sighed. It seemed to be her fate to talk about academics, when, for the first time in her life, all she could think about was a party.

CHAPTER SIX

Troy was sitting in the cafeteria with Chad and Zeke, enjoying his ham sandwich and feeling relaxed for the first time in at least a week. The basketball team had been practising the weave drill for the last few days, and it was looking really good. Everyone was pumped up for the first game of the season, with their archrivals, West High School.

"West High is going down!" Chad said. "Our new offence is lookin' sharp!"

"Those Knights won't know what hit them!" Zeke agreed, his eyes gleaming. "We're gonna be on fire this season, I can feel it! Play-offs, here we come!"

"Hold on, we haven't even played our first game yet," Troy protested, but he was smiling. He wouldn't admit it to anyone, not even Gabriella, but he couldn't help dreaming a little bit about winning another championship. Last year had been sweet, and he'd love to end his senior year in exactly the same way. "Remember what Coach always says—"

"Play one week at a time," Chad and Zeke said in perfect unison, and then they laughed.

"It doesn't hurt to dream about the future once in a while, though," Chad added.

"I guess not," Troy agreed, even though he felt it was all he thought about these days. His mind began to wander to one of the five books the careers counsellor had given him the day before. It was all about the new technologies used to solve crimes, and it had really sparked his imagination. In fact, he had only read three chapters before putting the book down and getting on the Internet to find out about colleges that offered criminal justice degrees.

"Did you guys know that a dentist once caught a criminal by comparing the guy's teeth to the bite marks in an apple left at the crime scene?" he said. He pulled his own apple out of his lunch bag, took a bite, then held it up to demonstrate his story. "Pretty cool, huh?"

Chad and Zeke exchanged puzzled glances, then shrugged.

"Listen. I just want to make some bite marks on these totally excellent chocolate chip cookies!" Zeke opened a plastic bag filled with cookies and offered them around. "I was in a baking mood last night," he explained.

"You're always in a baking mood," Chad said as he grabbed a cookie. "And I, for one, am grateful." He took a bite and closed his eyes in bliss. "Awesome, as always," he said, giving Zeke a high five.

Zeke nodded smugly. "My secret is adding an extra touch of brown sugar and then–"

"Hey, can I join you guys?" Gabriella interrupted. She was standing by their table, holding her lunch tray.

"Sure," Troy said, scooting over to give her room to sit down.

Zeke smiled and said hello, but Chad glanced over Gabriella's shoulder and opened his eyes wide in mock horror.

"Look out," he muttered. "The ice queen cometh!"

Everyone turned to see Sharpay confidently walking toward them.

"No worries," Zeke said cheerfully. "I will stave off her frosty wrath with my superdelicious chocolate chip cookie. It melts the coldest heart!"

They were still laughing when Sharpay got to their table.

"Hi!" she said brightly. "Are you guys ready for the Halloween party?"

Troy managed not to groan. Was that stupid party the only thing people could talk about?

"You bet!" Zeke said. "I already have a baker's jacket, of course, and I thought I'd bring a special batch of cinnamon cookies with me to hand out–"

"Yeah, great, cinnamon cookies are always a party hit," Sharpay said, cutting him off abruptly. She turned her high-beam smile on Troy. "But Troy, I really wanted to ask for *your* help."

"Ooh, cold," Chad muttered to a crestfallen Zeke.

"Help with what?" Troy asked warily.

"Well, it's more like I want your advice," she said sweetly. "I have several ideas for costumes and they're all so completely fabulous that I can't decide which one to choose!"

"Um, well . . ." Troy glanced wildly around the table for help, but Chad just grinned at him. Zeke was sulkily eating the last cookie. Gabriella was watching Sharpay with no expression on her face. "What kind of costumes are you thinking about?" Troy asked finally.

"At first, I thought that I would dress like a famous actress," Sharpay went on. "I mean, then I could get really dressed up and look totally glamorous. And I have a gold trophy that looks almost like a real Oscar that I could carry! But then I thought, is 'famous actress' just way too obvious? Maybe I should go as a Grammy-winning singer. But I also want my costume to represent my dancing talent—"

"Sure you don't want to work some puppetry into that costume?" Chad asked, feigning innocence. "Or – here's a great idea! – maybe a little mime?" He added, just to make the point clear, "You know mime artists don't *talk*."

"I'm sure it seems funny to someone with limited career options," she said loftily. "But deciding what to do with your life can be completely overwhelming when you're multitalented like me!"

"Yeah?" Chad said dryly. "Maybe you should try

to develop multiple personality disorder. Although the thought of five different Sharpays wandering through the halls—" He shuddered. "Man, I know it's Halloween, but I'm spooking myself!"

"I am not talking to you," she snapped. She took a deep breath and pointedly turned to smile at Troy. "So, Troy? Which costume do you think I should wear? Remember, I want to look absolutely *dazzling.*"

Troy couldn't help but return her smile. Chad always said that Sharpay was a total ice queen, but she had always been really friendly to Troy. . .

"They all sound great," he said.

"Really?" Sharpay actually batted her eyelashes. "That is so sweet of you! Thank you *so* much. I really value your opinion." She turned as if to go, then turned back. "What about you, Gabriella? What kind of costume are you wearing?"

Gabriella hesitated. "I haven't had a chance to think about it too much," she finally said. "I know I want to go into science, but I'm still trying to decide whether it would be more interesting to be a nuclear physicist or a biochemical engineer–"

"That sounds great," Sharpay interrupted, her voice ringing with insincerity. "And cheap. You could just borrow one of those white coats from the science lab, and you'd be good to go."

"Right," Gabriella said tersely. Those lab coats were one-size-fits-all, which meant that they were all miles too big for her. And most of them had at least one strange brownish stain somewhere. . .

"You wouldn't even have to spend any time doing your hair and make-up!" Sharpay went on cheerfully. "After all, women scientists don't need to worry about their looks, do they? Their pictures never end up in the tabloids and they're always busy doing, you know–" She waved one hand vaguely, "–science-y stuff."

She widened her eyes and added earnestly, "I almost envy you, Gabriella, I really do." She gave the table a big, bright smile and said, "Ta-ta for now!" and flounced off.

"She's probably going to wear something that looks like it belongs on a Broadway stage!" Chad said, shaking his head.

"Sharpay is a little obsessive about theatre," Troy agreed. "But it's kind of cool that she knows exactly what she wants to do."

He glanced over at Gabriella, who was frowning down at the meatloaf on her plate as if it had done her a personal wrong.

"Hey, are you okay?" he asked.

"Of course," she said, trying to smile. "I was just thinking about my own costume."

"Oh, right, the lab coat," Troy said vaguely. "That sounds great. Hey, did I tell you about what the careers counsellor told me?"

As he talked on, Gabriella kept smiling and nodding, but she didn't hear a word he said. She was too busy wondering how she could make a lab coat look *dazzling*.

* * *

That night, Gabriella stood in front of the full-length mirror in her bedroom and looked sadly at her reflection. She turned to one side, then the other, then shook her head. After half an hour of trying, she had to face the bitter truth. There was no way to make a lab coat look dazzling. Even *decent* was a bit of a stretch.

She could hear Sharpay's voice in her head: *"Women scientists don't need to worry about their looks, do they? They're always busy doing, you know – science-y stuff."*

Gabriella ripped the lab coat off and tossed it over a chair.

This is ridiculous, she thought. I have more important things to worry about than a silly party costume.

Then she remembered the way Sharpay had flirted with Troy in the cafeteria. And the way Troy had smiled back at her.

Actually, she thought, that's not true. In fact, the *most* important thing I have to worry about right now is that silly party costume.

CHAPTER SEVEN

Tension was high in the classroom where the SAT tutoring was taking place. Gabriella tried to look relaxed and confident as she began handing back the practice tests the students had taken a few days earlier.

"Now just remember, this was only the *first* practice test," she said cheerfully. "Everyone's going to have a lot more chances to work on taking the SATs in real time—"

"You're saying we did terribly, aren't you?"

START WITH THE
BASICS

The basketball players, brainiacs and actors at East High might not always get along or see eye to eye on everything, but there is one thing they can all agree on. Whether it's acting, athletics, or scholastic endeavors, to really become a pro you have to learn the fundamentals. With that in mind, HERE IS AN ESSENTIAL A-Z GUIDE that will give you all of the basics on East High!

A-Z

A

IS FOR ACTING. Sometimes boys act like they don't like girls that they really like. Other times girls act something isn't bothering them when something clearly is. Acting isn't always just for plays and musicals!

B

IS FOR BASKETBALL AND ALSO FOR BRAINIAC. The school brainiacs don't like to admit it, but basketball rules the school and the players are treated like heroes (at least as long as they continue to win!)

C

IS FOR CALLBACKS. Thanks to some keen manipulating by Sharpay, Troy and Gabriella almost missed the callbacks for Twinkle Towne.

D

is for Drama (see letter 'A') and also for Detention. While Chad, Troy and Gabriella are good kids, they all still get sent to detention now and again (for Chad, it's mostly again and again!)

E IS FOR EAST HIGH AND ELECTRIFYING. East High might just be another high school if it weren't for the electrifying talent of so many of its students – amazing athletes, stellar scholars and darling dramatists.

F F IS FOR FLIRTING. Between Troy and Gabriella, Chad and Taylor, Zeke chasing Sharpay and Sharpay trying to pry Troy away from Gabriella, there is no shortage of flirting going on at East High.

G IS FOR GYMNASIUM. The gymnasium is where Chad feels most at home in school. If he could he's spend every minute of the day there practising his basketball skills.

H IS FOR HARD WORK. No matter what endeavor you try – scholastics, athletics, drama, poetry readings, band competitions – success only comes with a lot of hard work.

I IS FOR INTELLIGENCE. Troy likes Gabriella because she is honest, kind, talented and willing to try new things. But he also really respects her intelligence and looks to her first when he needs help with an extracurricular poetry lesson for the basketball players.

J IS FOR JASON CROSS. Jason doesn't always get as much attention as the more outgoing and celebrated players on the basketball team like Chad and Troy, but he is an important part of the squad and always a source of comic relief!

K IS FOR KELSI NIELSEN. Kelsi might be soft-spoken and vertically challenged but she has a big heart and she's always willing to go the extra distance for her friends.

L IS FOR LAVA SPRINGS CLUB. The summer that Troy, Gabriella and the rest of their friends spent at Lava Springs was educational, to say the least. They all learned a lot about themselves and each other.

M

IS FOR MUSICALS AND MS DARBUS. While the Basketball and Scholastic Decathlon teams get a lot of attention, the school wouldn't be the same without its annual musicals and Ms Darbus' direction.

IS FOR NEW YEAR'S RESORT PARTY. Fate is funny sometimes. Gabriella and Troy both almost skipped the New Year's party at the resort they were staying at, and if they had they might never have discovered what great voices they had or how much fun it was to sing together.

N

IS FOR OVERACHIEVER. Troy can get himself into trouble when he tries to do everything — sometimes being the basketball captain, leader of the band, boyfriend, model employee, dutiful son and good friend doesn't leave a lot of time for just being, well, Troy!

O

IS FOR PRIMO BOY. Troy Bolton might be modest but that doesn't stop him from being the BMOC (Big Man On Campus)! This has not escaped Sharpay's attention, who believes that she and Troy are destined to be leading man and leading lady together.

IS FOR QUIZ. A quiz is a great way to test your knowledge of a subject. So once you think you are an expert of all things High School Musical, put your knowledge to the test with the great quizzes in this book and the other books in the Stories from East High series!

IS FOR RYAN EVANS. Where Sharpay goes you are almost guaranteed to see Ryan in her footsteps. But lately Ryan has begun to question how his sister does things and to take some initiative himself.

S IS FOR SCHOLASTIC DECATHLON. Once Taylor recruited Gabriella to the cause there was really no stopping the East High Scholastic team. The basketball team isn't the only champion in town.

T IS FOR TWINKLE TOWNE. If it hadn't been for the Winter Musical, Gabriella and Troy might never have gotten the chance to show just how talented they are.

U IS FOR UNBELIEVABLE. Even with a essential A-Z guide to use as a reference it's impossible to predict what adventures (and misadventures!) your favourite Wildcats will get into next!

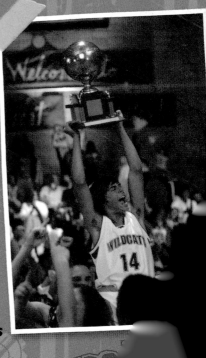

V IS FOR VICTORY. Between the basketball team and the Scholastic Decathlon team, there's an awful lot of winning going on at East High right now. And while the Drama Club doesn't measure anything in wins and losses, each production is kind of a victory too!

WILDCATS

W
IS FOR WILDCAT SPIRIT WEEK. **Sharpay looks forward to this week almost as much as opening nights, spring break and Christmas, because it gives her a chance to prove that she is the best of the best!**

X
IS FOR XS AND OS. **Even with great talent, a basketball team still needs sound strategy and that's where Coach Bolton comes in. He teaches the players as well as motivating them to succeed.**

Y
IS FOR YEARBOOK. **The East High yearbook always captures the annual highlights – who excelled, who flopped, who has the most talent, who is crushing on who, who is most likely to wear a funky hat, headband or bake an exceptional custard.**

Z
FOR ZEKE'S PASTRIES. **Not everyone was happy when ~~h~~e first told people that he had a secret passion for ~~bakin~~g, but after trying out one of his pastries they ~~s~~oon won over!**

Ryan said. He put his head down on the table, a picture of despair.

"No, no!" Gabriella said quickly. "Some of the scores were very high—"

"Really?" Nathan said. "What was the highest score? And who got it?"

"I'm not sure that's important—" she started to say, but Ryan interrupted her.

"You said *some* of the scores were high," he pointed out. "But not all of them, right? If some of them were *high*, that means other scores were *low*, isn't that what you're really saying? I knew it, I knew I would fail. I'm no good at tests. I get too freaked out and then all the words start blurring on the page and I get lightheaded and I can't breathe and—"

"Calm down, Ryan!" Sharpay snapped.

"Yeah, there's only room for one drama queen in the Evans family!" Chad joked.

Sharpay glared at him. "I am *not* a drama queen!"

Most people tried their best not to laugh. Only a few succeeded.

Nathan raised his hand. "What was the lowest score?"

"I really don't think that's important," Gabriella said coolly.

"I disagree," Nathan said. "That information could be absolutely vital to our success! In fact, I think you should plot our scores on a bell curve and compare them to the average distribution of scores on the nationwide test."

Gabriella stared at him, openmouthed. *Are you crazy?* she wanted to yell. But she settled for taking a deep breath and saying, "I don't have time to do that. Besides, the most important thing is to study hard and do the best you can—"

"No, the important thing is to get the highest score!" Nathan insisted. "To blow out the bell curve! To wreak havoc with college admission standards! To be the last man standing when the invigilator says, 'Pencils down!'"

Complete silence greeted this remark.

Then Chad murmured, "Dude, I just want to

be the last man standing at the Enchilada Express all-you-can-eat buffet."

Gabriella gave Chad a warning look as she continued handing back the tests. Nathan pursed his lips when he saw his score. "Mmm," he murmured. "Better. But not good enough!"

He fixed his gaze on Gabriella. "Don't you think it's about time these tutoring sessions switched into high gear?" he complained. "Maybe you should set up a fast track for some of the, um . . . well, *brighter* students here?"

"We're all here to help each other," Gabriella said. Her voice was calm, even though she was becoming more and more frustrated. "If you've already mastered the material, maybe you could teach somebody else what you know."

Nathan rolled his eyes at that idea. "I guess I'll just have to work harder on my own," he grumbled. He pulled out his digital organizer and began tapping keys. "Let's see, if I spend an extra hour each night going over my calculus notes, and get up thirty minutes earlier each morning to practise verbal comprehension exercises . . ."

Ryan quickly peeked at Nathan's test paper. "Twenty-three eighty!" he whispered in awe. "You must be a genius."

"Highly probable," Nathan agreed. "Almost certain, in fact."

"*Or* you're very good at taking tests," Gabriella said. As she handed Ryan his test, she added, "Not all geniuses are, you know. Einstein got terrible grades when he was in school–"

But Ryan wasn't listening. "I knew it," he whispered to himself as he looked at his score. "I knew I was freaking out too much when I was taking the test! I totally panicked! I always do!"

"Nerves have nothing to do with it," Nathan said to Ryan. "Some people are born with brains, like me. Some aren't."

Like you. The unspoken words hovered in the air.

Gabriella came to a halt in the middle of the aisle, her dark eyes snapping with anger. She had recently spent a month or so tutoring Ryan in algebra. She saw how hard he worked, even though maths clearly wasn't his strength. He had even high-fived her in the hall after making a B- on his last test. She wasn't going to let this little pipsqueak Nathan James destroy Ryan's confidence like that! Even Sharpay – well, maybe she wasn't the top student at East High, but that didn't give Nathan the right to sneer at her, either!

She said quickly, "That's ridiculous. Plenty of supersmart people slide by in school because they know they can. And other people who work harder actually end up learning a lot more because it didn't come easily."

"Just like basketball," Chad chimed in. "Hard work can beat natural talent any day of the week."

Nathan gave an irritating little laugh. "Yeah, you keep believing that if it makes you feel better," he said smugly. "Luckily, I have talent *and* I work hard. Constantly, in fact. Around the clock."

"Oh, you even study when you're sleeping?" Chad asked mockingly. "That's dedication, dude!"

Nathan's face darkened. "As a matter of fact, yes."

He pulled a CD out of his backpack. "Have you seen these 'learn while you sleep' CDs? You put on some headphones when you get into bed, let the CD play all night, and when you get up – voilá! You're at least twenty points smarter! Twenty-four hundred, here I come!"

"Oh, please!" Sharpay stood up abruptly and slung her backpack over her shoulder. "I really can't waste any more time here," she announced. "I must get to rehearsal!"

Her brother looked puzzled. "Rehearsal? Ms Darbus hasn't even decided what the fall show is going to be–"

"Exactly!" she snapped. "I am going to rehearse the lead roles for the three musicals she is thinking about putting on so we can find the part that is perfect for me." She flashed an insincere smile at Gabriella. "Sorry I can't keep coming to your little class, but the theatre must always come first with me!"

"Oh. Well, okay." Gabriella wasn't sure whether she should try to talk Sharpay into staying, because that's what a good tutor would do, or smile and let her go, because that would be the easiest thing to do. Before she could make up her mind, Principal Matsui walked through the door, beaming and rubbing his hands with delight.

"So, how is everything going?" he asked. "Are we all on the road to victory?"

"Actually," Sharpay said, "I'm on the road out that door. So, if you'll excuse me—"

"Hold on!" Principal's Matsui's eyebrows raised in surprise. "You're leaving the SAT tutoring session?"

Sharpay stopped, but only because the principal was standing directly in her path. "Yes," she said haughtily. "In fact, I'm leaving for good."

Gabriella stepped in quickly. "It turns out that Sharpay has a, um, scheduling conflict."

"I think the sessions were a great idea,"

Sharpay said sweetly. "For *other* people, that is. But Ms Darbus desperately needs my help!"

"Hmm." The principal's eyes narrowed. He saw the practice test that Sharpay was still clutching. "May I take a look at that?"

She reluctantly handed the paper over. Prinicpal Matusi glanced at it, then closed his eyes for a moment, as if in pain. Before he could say anything, however, Sharpay jumped in. "I really must get to the school hall," she said. "Ta ta!" And she sailed out of the door.

Gabriella watched her go with a feeling of relief. Then the principal said, "Gabriella, perhaps I could speak to you in the hall for a moment?" He turned to the class and waved a hand. "The rest of you carry on with your studying. This will only take a minute."

Gabriella's stomach jumped a little as she followed the principal out of the door. Even though she liked Mr Matsui, it always sounded faintly ominous when a principal asked you to step into the hall.

He turned to her and said, "Gabriella, you can't let Sharpay give up on the tutoring after only one week."

"But I can't make her attend if she doesn't want to," she protested. "It's a voluntary group!"

"Oh, I'm sure you can persuade Sharpay to return to the fold," he said breezily. "And it's absolutely vital that you do so." He looked down at the test he was holding and shook his head. "She's smart enough to do quite well, but all she ever thinks about is being onstage. With scores like these, she could significantly lower our school average – all by herself."

He smiled at her, and added more cheerfully, "But if anyone is up to the challenge of getting Sharpay to focus on this test, Gabriella, it's you! So, best of luck – and, remember, keep me posted on how things are going."

CHAPTER EIGHT

Two days later, Gabriella still hadn't talked to Sharpay about rejoining the tutoring sessions. The fact was, she dreaded Sharpay's response, which was sure to give a whole new meaning to the word 'drama'. Still, the amount of time left before the SATs was dwindling rapidly. She couldn't avoid the conversation any longer.

As she was walking toward the chemistry lab, she saw Sharpay standing in the hall and staring intently into her locker. Dozens of students swirled around her, but she didn't seem to notice them. Gabriella took a deep breath and headed her way.

As she got closer, she saw that Sharpay was making a series of strange faces. First, she would open her mouth and eyes as wide as they could go. Then, she would narrow her eyes and frown. Then, she stretched her mouth into an odd grimace. And through all of this, Sharpay's eyes remained riveted on something inside her locker.

Curious about what could possibly be fascinating enough to hold Sharpay's attention for so long, Gabriella peered over her shoulder and saw—

Oh. Of course. Sharpay had glued a mirror to the back of her locker.

She caught sight of Gabriella's reflection behind her, and turned. "Oh, hello there," she said coolly.

"Um . . . sorry to interrupt your, um . . . well, whatever it was you were doing," Gabriella said.

"Acting exercises," Sharpay said in a snooty voice. "Designed to strengthen the facial muscles and add to the expressiveness of one's instrument."

"Ah." Gabriella wanted to grin – it was such an *actorly* thing to call your face or body 'your instrument' – but she managed to nod soberly, as if she had just learned something very important. "Well, I don't mean to get in the way of your process, but I wanted to ask you–"

She stopped, suddenly aware of the bareness of Sharpay's locker. "Excuse me, but where are all your books?"

Sharpay smirked. "In my locker annexe, of course." She opened the door next to her locker. A stack of textbooks was inside. "Ms Darbus pulled a few strings for me. I mean, it's really no different than a star having a private dressing room is it?"

"I guess not," Gabriella said. "Anyway, what I wanted to ask you was if you would consider coming back to the tutoring session."

Sharpay stared at her blankly. "Why in the world would I do that?"

"Because the sessions might help you get a better score?" Even to Gabriella's own ears, she didn't sound convincing at all.

"I don't need any help. Thanks, anyway," Sharpay sniffed. She swung the door of her locker annex, which closed with a clang.

Gabriella took a deep breath and started again. "Look, maybe you don't need help studying. But if you're nervous about taking the SATs, a little bit of practice will make you feel more confident. . . ."

"Nervous? Me?" Sharpay looked utterly dumbfounded at the thought. "I've stood centre stage with a blinding hot spotlight shining on me in front of an audience of hundreds, knowing that an entire production rested on my shoulders, and I didn't even blink!" She took one last glimpse at her mirrored reflection, then gently shut the locker door before turning back to Gabriella. "I have never had even one second of stage fright."

"Then what's the problem?" Gabriella asked, exasperated. "Why do you keep scoring so badly on the practice tests? And why don't you want to stick with the tutoring sessions?"

"Because I have bigger things on my mind!" Sharpay snapped.

"Like what?" Gabriella heard herself snap back.

"Acting, of course!" Sharpay said, shocked. "I am devoted to my art! It takes an enormous amount of dedication to nurture my talent! I can't waste time memorizing formulas and answering multiple-choice questions and writing essays!" She paused, then added, "I mean, that's what brainiacs do."

Gabriella opened her mouth, then quickly thought better of what she was about to say. Instead, she closed it, took a deep breath, and counted to ten. Then she said, in as calm a voice as she could muster, "That's true. I can see that acting like a brainiac might be a bit of a stretch for you."

Sharpay's head whipped around. She glared at Gabriella. "And what do you mean by that?"

"I mean, actors have to learn to play parts that are very different from their real personalities," Gabriella said sweetly. "In your career, you might end up having to play an evil enchantress, for example, or a humble servant, or something."

"I know that!" Sharpay snapped.

"So the part of, er, brainiac might be a little much for you right now, that's all," Gabriella went on smoothly. "You shouldn't feel bad about it, Sharpay. You're only in high school, after all. You can't be expected to meet every acting challenge right away—"

"I can play any part, anywhere, at any time!" Sharpay cried.

"Really?" Gabriella put just the lightest touch of skepticism in her voice.

Sharpay scowled. "Are you doubting my acting ability?"

"Well . . ." Gabriella hesitated artfully before

adding, "I guess I'd believe you could act the part if I actually saw it. . . "

"And you will!" Sharpay drew herself up and added with great dignity, "And your little SAT tutoring session shall be my stage!"

"Excellent." Gabriella smiled with satisfaction. "I'll look forward to your performance."

"Of course you will," Sharpay replied haughtily. Then she hesitated, and a shadow of a doubt passed over her face. "I'll need to do some research, though. I've never played this part before. . . "

"Right," Gabriella said, smiling. "But *I've* played it all my life."

Sharpay nodded slowly, then smiled at Gabriella. "Yes," she said in a considered tone. "You would be the perfect person for me to shadow as research for my role!"

"Exactly," Gabriella said. "So, let's get started. . . "

CHAPTER NINE

What do you think of my new glasses?"
Sharpay turned her head this way and that so
Gabriella could check out the horn-rimmed
frames perched on the end of her nose.

"They look very nice," Gabriella said. "But . . .
since when do you need glasses?"

Sharpay's gaze strayed to one of the five mir-
rors in her large, airy bedroom, where they had
gone after school to study. "Oh, I don't need
them to *see*," she said, cocking her head to one

side and frowning a bit as she judged the effect. "I need them to get into my role."

"Your role?" Gabriella wondered if she had missed something.

"You know! The role of *great student*," Sharpay said. "Actors have to do more than just learn lines! They have to research their characters' lives! If you're playing a police officer, you go out on patrol with real policemen. If you're playing a figure skater, you take skating lessons. And if you're playing someone who aces the SATs—"

"Oh, right, I've read about actors doing that."

"So," Sharpay said, all business, "the first thing I have to do is interview you about what your life as a total brainiac is like, then I have to copy it, down to the smallest detail."

Gabriella grinned. "You're going to copy *everything*? Even the way I spend days writing an essay or how I double-check every calculation in my chemistry homework?"

Sharpay looked a little unnerved at this, but she quickly rallied. "Everything," she said firmly. "I will do whatever I must to really live this role! After all, great art requires great sacrifice."

"Okay, then." Gabriella, pleased, opened the SAT prep book to the first page. This couldn't have gone better if she had scripted it herself! "The first thing I would do is read through these tips about taking the test. . . "

Ryan sat cross-legged on his bedroom floor. The lights were dim, the curtains closed, the air silent and still. He put his palms together, closed his eyes and tried to centre himself.

After a long, long moment, he realized that finding his centre might take more time than he had available. After all, the SATs were only one week away – and, despite all the tutoring sessions and practice tests, he was getting steadily more nervous, not less.

Luckily, he had once played the part of a Buddhist monk in an experimental play that Ms Darbus had directed at the community theatre.

He remembered that his character had always been serene, despite being murdered by a zombie monkey right before the intermission and then wandering through the rest of the play as a ghost (and, even worse, as a ghost with no lines).

As worried as he was about failing the SATs, Ryan figured that being killed by a zombie monkey was an even more terrible fate. So he struck a match and lit the three candles that he had placed next to a plate of pears (the monk character had been very big on fruit).

He took a deep breath and began chanting: "Om-nee-oh-mee-ah! Om-nee-oh-mee-ah! Om-nee-oh-mee—"

"Aaahhhh!" As if in response, there was a scream from next door.

Ryan jumped. Had his chanting awakened some evil spirit? Had he stirred up powerful forces in the universe that should have been left alone? Had he somehow really summoned some ancient zombie—

The door flew open. An ancient zombie stood at the entrance to his room!

Ryan tried to scream but could only whimper.

"Would you please shut up!" the ancient zombie yelled. "How is a person supposed to study with that racket going on in here?"

Ryan looked more closely. Oh. It was just Sharpay – but why did she look so terrible? She had some kind of mud caked on her face; her hair was hanging down in lank strands; she was wearing faded old sweats; and there were glasses perched on her nose.

"You look awful," he said.

"That's because I'm being *studious*," his sister snarled. "And the only spa treatment I could squeeze in between my geometry- and history-review time was a facial mask, which is the bare minimum for maintaining my high standard of beauty! I'll just have time to scrape it off before it's time to write my English essay! And I can't do any of that with proper focus and concentration when you're howling *at the top of your lungs!*"

"I wasn't howling–" he began meekly, but, before he could finish, she had slammed the door and stomped back to her room.

Ryan stared at the closed door for a moment, then shrugged. So he couldn't chant – fortunately, he still remembered the meditation exercise he had done every night before taking the stage. He took a bite out of a pear and closed his eyes, focusing on the taste of the fruit and letting go of all external thoughts. . . .

Fifteen minutes later, he opened his eyes and realized that he felt relaxed and calm and . . . serene!

He caught sight of his SAT prep book, which was sitting on his desk waiting to be cracked open, and he was thrilled to realize that he didn't feel even the slightest flutter of nerves.

"Once again, theatre has come to the rescue!" he whispered to the still, silent room. Then he closed his eyes again. The SAT prep book could wait. Ryan thought a little more meditation was in order . . .

* * *

"Okay, let's try that again," Troy called out to the team. He was sweating, and it wasn't just because they'd been practising the same drill for twenty minutes. His dad had been called into a last-minute faculty meeting and had told Troy to supervise the practice.

Which wouldn't have been a big deal – he was the team captain, after all – except that the practice was going so very, very badly. The team kept running the weave drill, and Jason Cross kept looping back and catching the pass from Chad before sending it flying Troy's way – and each and every time, Troy had dropped the ball.

"Hey, man, maybe we should take a break," Zeke suggested. "You seem kind of out of it."

"No, no, I'm fine," Troy said. "Come on, one more time–"

He tossed the ball to Chad, who dribbled down the court and did a behind-the-back pass to Jason, who looped back and tossed it to Troy . . .

. . . who got his hands on it. But then it slipped from his fingers, and he dropped it. Again.

"Aggh." He leaned over, his hands on his knees, and groaned with frustration.

Chad and Zeke trotted over, looking concerned.

"Hey, what's going on, Troy?" Chad asked. "Your head's not in the game today."

"I know, I know. . . ." Troy tried not to snap at his friend. It was painfully obvious to everyone in the gym that he wasn't playing well today!

"Maybe you just need to chill out for a few minutes," Zeke suggested. "Try to think about something else. Something besides basketball, I mean."

Troy walked over to the stands and sat down. "That's the problem," he said. "I'm thinking about too many things, and none of them have anything to do with basketball!"

"What's on your mind, bro?" Chad asked, looking puzzled.

"Well, here's the thing . . ." Troy said slowly.

"Remember when I went to the careers counsellor?"

"How could we forget?" Jason rolled his eyes. "First, we heard all about how great forensic science is, then we listened to you go on and on about whether you should become a psychologist. And then you told us all about the various branches of oceanography—"

"Yeah, well, I was talking to Ms Johnson yesterday," Troy interrupted. "She said my maths grades are good enough to think about engineering. But last Thanksgiving, my uncle told me that the future is in computers. But then I saw this cool documentary on TV, and I got kind of interested in archaeology. Digging up ancient burial grounds seems really cool—"

"Yeah, if you don't mind getting hit with an ancient curse," Zeke said darkly.

Chad was shaking his head. "I have a better idea. Look towards the future! How about video games?"

"Hey, I hadn't thought about that," Troy said.

"After all, someone needs to design all those games. . . ."

"Exactly my point," Chad said smugly.

Zeke looked at Troy shrewdly. "So this is why you're zero for twelve in free throws today?" he asked.

"Yeah," Troy admitted. "I guess I've kind of lost focus."

"You're taking this stuff way too seriously," Chad said. He tossed the ball to Troy. "Come on. If you're going to obsess about your future, then visualize yourself as a *basketball player*."

Troy grinned. "Yeah, you're right. Let's get back to work."

But as he dribbled down the court, his mind kept drifting. Maybe, he thought, I should do some volunteer work at the hospital and see if I want to be a doctor. . . .

"What are you doing, Troy? Shoot!" Zeke yelled.

Startled, Troy stopped and threw the ball . . . which bounced off the rim with a clang.

He sighed. I'd better start focusing, he thought, or my future definitely won't include basketball.

"Quit staring at me!" Gabriella said.

"I have to! I'm researching my role!" Sharpay replied. "Just act the way you normally would. Forget I'm even here!"

Gabriella sighed. How was she supposed to forget that Sharpay was sitting across the table from her in study hall, her eyes following every move Gabriella made? And then there were all those notes! Every time Gabriella opened a book, or scribbled down a chemistry equation, or filled in a worksheet on French verb tenses, Sharpay would write down what she had done and murmur something to herself, like, "I must remember that!" or, "Excellent character gesture!"

Gabriella was beginning to have enormous sympathy for zoo animals.

She stared at her calculus textbook, trying to absorb the information on the page. She had been reading the same section over and over for the last ten minutes without understanding a single word.

She sighed heavily.

"What's wrong?" Sharpay whispered.

"Nothing!" Gabriella said.

"But you just sighed," Sharpay said. "How are you feeling right this minute, as you head into the second hour of studying for tomorrow's calculus test?"

"I feel fine!" Gabriella snapped.

Sharpay frowned slightly. "Can you be more specific? I don't think I can act that."

Gabriella gritted her teeth and reminded herself that she should be glad that Sharpay was taking this so seriously. "I feel," she said carefully, "like I've been reading the same section over and over without understanding a word. So now I am going to do some of the sample problems at the end of the chapter to see if that helps me understand this equation."

"Ohhh, okay." Sharpay nodded happily and scribbled a note to herself.

"Now, if you want to really feel the emotion here," Gabriella added craftily, "you should study for that geometry test you told me you have next week."

"Great idea," Sharpay said. "That will really help me get inside the character."

She flipped open her textbook and began reading.

As Gabriella began tapping numbers into her calculator, she went over the amazing changes that her experiment had wrought in seven short days.

For the last week, Sharpay had been studying two or three hours a night. She had attended every SAT tutoring session and then stayed after for extra practice. In her regular classes, she had begun raising her hand any time a teacher asked the class a question. And she had gone on a strict "brain food" diet of fish, chicken, fruit and vegetables.

Word had spread throughout the school. Teachers wondered if the real Sharpay had been replaced by a long-lost twin. Principal Matsui was beside himself with glee. And Nathan James was getting more and more annoyed as Sharpay's score got better with every practice test she took.

At the thought of Nathan, Gabriella relaxed a little. She even smiled. Because if it was satisfying to see Sharpay working so hard, it was even more satisfying to watch Nathan's theory of natural genius completely collapse.

"Hello, everyone," Sharpay said in a sober, measured voice. She stood next to the cafeteria table where Gabriella and Taylor had settled in for a lunchtime chat. "May I join you for lunch?"

"Um, sure," Taylor said, shooting Gabriella a confused look. "But why are you talking like that? And why are you *dressed* like that?"

Sharpay's hair was pulled back into a neat bun and she had her glasses on. She was wearing a knee-length navy skirt, a navy blazer, a white cotton shirt buttoned to the top, and low-heeled navy shoes.

"You look like an accountant," Taylor continued, ignoring Gabriella's nudge under the table.

"Looks aren't important," Sharpay said. "Brains are."

"Although you do look very nice," Gabriella hastened to add. "How did you do on your geometry test?"

"Aced it," Sharpay said simply.

Taylor's mouth hung open. "You . . . aced . . . a *geometry* test?"

Sharpay nodded complacently. "But I'm a little worried about history," she said. "That's why I wanted to sit with you two."

"Excuse me?" Now Taylor looked beyond confused. She looked positively befuddled. "What does eating lunch with us have to do with history?"

"It's one of the seven habits of highly successful students, right, Gabriella?" Sharpay said. "If you hang out with smart people, you'll subconsciously absorb the way they think and behave and learn and you'll become smarter yourself."

"Interesting theory." Taylor flashed Gabriella an impish grin. "Maybe you should write a book, Gabriella!"

"It's just a part of the experiment Sharpay and I are conducting," Gabriella said quickly. "I think I'll get dessert after all. Anyone want anything?"

"No, thanks." Sharpay already had her nose buried in her history textbook. "I need to spend every free minute reading about the Civil War!"

"I'll go with you," Taylor said, jumping out of her seat. As she walked with Gabriella to the lunch line, she whispered, "You better watch out, girl. I think you've created a monster!"

"Think positive," Troy whispered to himself as he stood on the free-throw line. "You can do this. Take it easy. And . . ."

He launched the basketball through the air.

Bing! It bounced off the rim.

Troy groaned. Free throws used to be a piece

of cake for him! Even during a hard-fought game, nothing ever rattled him. Now he couldn't seem to hit a single shot, even when he was just practising by himself in an empty gym.

Gritting his teeth, he grabbed the ball and went back to the free-throw line to try again.

"Come on," he whispered. "You've done this a million times. . . ."

Thunk! This time, the ball hit the backboard.

"Aarggh!' he yelled as he dived for the ball.

"Everything all right in here?"

Troy turned to see his dad standing in the gym door, watching him with a worried expression on his face.

"Fine," he muttered. He looked down and bounced the ball a few times. Even that felt off-rhythm now!

"Okay." His dad walked over to where he stood. "Getting in a little free-throw practice, huh?"

"Yeah." Troy hesitated, then looked up at his father. "I really need it, too. I think I've lost my game."

"I doubt that," his father said, smiling slightly. "But you have seemed a little . . . well, worried lately."

Troy nodded, but didn't say anything.

"Anything you want to talk about?"

"Well . . ." Troy shrugged. "I'm getting a little freaked out, I guess. About my future."

"You're only seventeen," his dad said, puzzled. "What's the problem?"

"Exactly! I'm seventeen! That's the problem!" Troy said. "I'll be going to college next year, and I have to figure out where I'm going and what I'm going to major in and what career I'm going to have and everything I'll be doing for the rest of my life!"

His dad looked startled. "Hey, what brought this on?"

"It's that Halloween party," Troy said. "I thought I had my future all mapped out, but now I'm not so sure!"

"Oh, that." His dad chuckled. "You know, the Student Council has very good intentions. It's not a bad idea to start thinking about your life. But, Troy—" He shook his head. "Most college students change their major several times. And the average person changes careers four times in his or her life! So the idea that you'll know right now what you want to do – well, you're putting too much pressure on yourself. Just start paying attention to subjects that interest you. Try them out and see if you like them. If you don't, try something else."

"That's all there is to it?" Troy asked. His dad made it sound so simple.

"Pretty much," his dad nodded. "Look at me. Loved basketball. Loved playing basketball. But could I make it my career?" He shook his head. "No way. But I started doing some volunteer coaching and found out that I loved that, too, so I got my education degree. If you don't spend too much time trying to figure out what you *should* be, I guarantee you'll find out what you *want* to be."

"Really?" Troy couldn't believe the sense of

relief that swept through his body. Then he said, "But what about that scout? I know you want me to get a basketball scholarship—"

"Whoa, hold on!" His dad held out his hands as if to stop the flow of Troy's words. "It would be great if you could get a scholarship, but if that doesn't happen, no big deal. Everything will work out — unless you keep worrying so much that you don't enjoy your senior year. Got it?"

Troy smiled. "Got it. Thanks, Dad."

"That's what I'm here for," his dad said. "Now, let me give you a little tip about how to focus when you're shooting free throws. . . ."

CHAPTER TEN

"**W**ildcats are number one! Straight to the top!" The cheerleaders' chant rang through the gym.

Troy huddled with the team on the sidelines, listening as the coach – his dad – gave last-minute instructions.

"Relax out there, guys," Coach Bolton said. "Remember, just like practice."

"Just like practice," the players repeated.

"We are the best! Wildcats fight non-stop!" The cheerleaders had the crowd on its feet.

"Let's go, let's fight! We're here to win tonight!" Now people in the crowd were stomping their feet and clapping their hands. The noise boomed through the gym as the cheerleaders cartwheeled their way across the floor.

"Yay, Wildcats!" they yelled, shaking their pom-poms.

Then the teams met at centre court and the game was on.

Two hours later, Troy led the team in a rousing Wildcats victory cheer. The crowd was still screaming as they headed for the locker room, making plans about where they'd go for burgers after cleaning up. Just as he was about to leave the gym, a man wearing a suit and tie stopped him.

"Troy Bolton?"

"Yes, sir?" Troy looked the man up and down and knew who he was. The scout.

"Mac Johnson," he said. "I'm a scout for the University of Arizona. You played a good game tonight."

"Thanks."

His dad came up at that moment and shook Mac Johnson's hand.

"Good to see you," he said, beaming. "Especially on a night like this."

"An impressive win, coach. Keep it up and the Wildcats will win the championship again," the scout said. "I just wanted to offer my congratulations. And let you know that I'm keeping my eye on this young man."

"Good to hear it," Coach Bolton said. "I'm sure he'll be worth watching."

As Mac Johnson walked away, Troy's dad turned to him. "You did a great job tonight. Now I want you to forget what a great job you did, understand?"

"Um . . . no," Troy said, puzzled.

His dad grinned. "I want you to completely forget about the game, the scout and what your future may hold. Just go out with your friends and enjoy yourself. Got it?"

"Absolutely," Troy said, nodding.

* * *

Gabriella was surrounded by everyone who had participated in her SAT tutoring sessions. They stood nervously in the hall, waiting to be ushered into the classroom where the SATs would be administered.

"Now, remember what we talked about," she said. "On the multiple-choice questions, if you can eliminate two of the choices–"

"Go ahead and guess," Sharpay interrupted. "You have a fifty-fifty chance of getting the right answer."

"Exactly," Gabriella said. "And if there's a question you just don't understand–"

"Skip it and move on," Chad said.

"Right. And if you start to feel nervous–"

"Close your eyes, take deep breaths, and imagine that your mind is a clear, cloudless sky," Ryan said. He was carrying a small flower and had a blissful expression on his face.

"Um . . . sure," Gabriella said. "Why not?"

"This is amateur hour!" Nathan sniffed in disdain as he rooted around in his backpack. He pulled out a calculator, which he held reverentially in front of him. "Did I show you the new calculator my dad bought for me? It's an official licensed product of Ace the Test, Inc.! It has more power than the computers that run the space shuttle!"

Gabriella rolled her eyes and then turned to face the rest of the group. "Good luck, you guys! And remember, we're going out for pizza when we're done!"

Hours later, they were all still high-fiving each other and talking excitedly about how good they felt about the test. All except for Nathan, of course, who obsessively reworked math problems on his calculator and kept muttering, "I know I messed up on that distribution curve! And I lost it on the reading comprehension! I can't believe I'll have to take the test *again*!"

They were each on their second slice of pizza when Sharpay noticed that Gabriella wasn't as excited as everyone else.

"Did you freak out on the test?" she asked sympathetically. "Don't worry, it happens to everyone. I'm sure if you keep studying, you'll do better next time."

Gabriella couldn't help but laugh. This must be what it's like when an actor really gets into her role, she thought. Now Sharpay is giving *me* advice on taking tests! "It's not that," she said. "It's my stupid Halloween costume. Everyone else is going to look awesome! And I'm going to look—" She stopped, embarrassed.

But Ryan had been listening in. He cocked his head to one side. "You're going to look what?"

"Sharpay said it weeks ago. I really do want to be a scientist, so I guess I'm going to have to settle for looking, you know—" Gabriella shrugged. "*Drab.*"

Sharpay and Ryan gave each other a knowing look.

"No, you're not," Sharpay said.

"Not when you have *us* on your side!" Ryan agreed.

CHAPTER ELEVEN

"**H**ey, what an awesome costume!"

"That's so cool!"

"I've never seen anything like that before!"

As Gabriella walked into the gym where the Halloween party was in full swing, heads began to turn. She could hear the interested buzz as people pointed and stared. Sharpay and Ryan walked a few steps behind her, beaming proudly.

"Wow, Gabriella, that's like—" Taylor, elegantly dressed in her fitted suit and high heels, stood in front of her, wide-eyed. "Well, I'm not sure what it's like, but it's great!"

Just then, Troy bounded through the door and came to an abrupt stop in front of Gabriella as well. "You look . . . amazing!" he said. "I don't know what you're supposed to be, but you look *amazing*."

Gabriella giggled as she turned around slowly. She was wearing a long, silk, black dress that just grazed her ankles. Cords of flashing green lights had been wound around her body. More flashing lights – white this time – had been coiled through her hair, which was piled on top of her head.

"Come on, can't you guess?" she teased. "Take a look at the lights. Notice anything about the pattern?"

Taylor studied her for a few moments, biting her lip in thought. Suddenly, she grinned. "It's a double helix! You're a strand of DNA!"

"Wow." Chad and Zeke had joined them at this point. "That's supercreative."

"Well, it wasn't my idea." Gabriella pointed to

Sharpay and Ryan. "It was all theirs. I would have just settled for a lab coat, but they took the concept of scientist to a whole new level! And this is so much more fun!"

"It was nothing, really," Sharpay said airily.

"Once Gabriella explained what DNA was," her brother added.

Zeke looked from Sharpay to Ryan and back again. "You guys look really decked out," he said.

Ryan was wearing a black top hat, a starched white tuxedo shirt, tuxedo pants, and a flowing black cape. He bowed. "The Phantom of the Opera, at your service. That role has my name all over it! Broadway, here I come!"

Sharpay smiled shyly at Zeke and fluttered her fan in front of her face. "Why, thank you, kind sir," she said in a syrupy Southern drawl. "Do you know who I am?"

"Vivien Leigh in *Gone with the Wind*," he said.

Her eyes widened with surprise. "Yes! I finally decided that I should dress as a screen icon, in honour of what I hope to achieve someday. But . . . how did you know?"

He grinned as he matched her drawl. "Frankly, my dear, it's my favourite movie." He doffed his toque. "May I have this dance?"

They swept off to the dance floor. Ryan corralled Chad and Taylor to try out the haunted house. And Gabriella and Troy were left alone with one another.

"I'm glad you like my costume," Gabriella said shyly. "I was afraid that I was going to look like, you know . . . a drudge."

Troy laughed. "You? Never!"

She blushed. "Well, it helps that Ryan has such a wild imagination. And that Sharpay has a closet the size of a small bedroom, stuffed with costumes and props!" She hesitated, taking in his clothes for the first time. "But, um, if you don't mind me asking . . ."

"What am I dressed as?" Troy grinned. He was wearing jeans, a blue cotton shirt, and dress shoes.

"Well, yes." She smiled, puzzled. "I mean, you look really nice. But you also look completely . . . *normal.*"

"Exactly!" He took her elbow and began steering her toward the dance floor. "After talking to my dad, I realized that I was getting all freaked out about my costume because I thought that I had to have my whole future figured out right now."

The band started playing a slow song. He pulled Gabriella into his arms.

"So how did you decide what to wear?" she asked, smiling up at him as they began swaying to the music.

He shrugged. "I decided that I may not know *what* I want to be in the future, but I know *who* I want to be – me. So here's the future Troy. Just an ordinary guy."

"Nice to meet you, future Troy," she said. "And I don't think you're ordinary at all."

Something new is on the way!
Look for the next book in the Disney High
School Musical: Stories from East High series . . .

BROADWAY DREAMS

By N.B. Grace
Based on the Disney Channel Original Movie
"High School Musical", written by Peter Barsocchini

"**C**lass! Settle down! Settle, please!" Ms Darbus tried, in vain, to quieten the room. Everyone who was going on the big senior class trip – this year it was to New York City! – had gathered, and she could barely make herself heard over the din. Ms Darbus yelled again, "I need quiet, please!"

But the noise continued – until Coach Bolton stepped forward, put two fingers in his mouth and let out an ear-piercing whistle.

Instantly, the room went silent. "That's better!" he said. "Now. I know you are all excited about this trip, but let me make one thing clear: Ms Darbus and I are your chaperones, which means we are responsible for your safety, which means that when one of us says to settle down, you had better settle! Understood?"

Everyone nodded meekly.

"Excellent. Ms Darbus, you have the floor."

"Oh, well . . . thank you, Coach Bolton," the drama teacher said. "Indeed, we are about to embark on a grand journey together, an adventure that none of us will ever forget, a trip that will live on in our memories forever–"

Chad Danforth grinned at his buddy Troy Bolton, then pretended to snore.

"And that's not all! I have some very exciting news!" she continued, grandly ignoring him. "All of you have heard of *Last Bell!*, I hope?"

Most of the students looked puzzled, but Ryan Evans' hand shot into the air. "Yes, of course!" he cried out. "It's one of the most successful

Broadway musicals over the last five years!"

"Oh, how could I have missed that?" Chad asked, rolling his eyes.

"It's set in a high school, just like this one," Ryan went on. "I know all the songs by heart!" He got a faraway look in his eyes and added dreamily, "Sometimes I imagine what it would be like to appear on Broadway in a show like that. I could do it, I know I could–"

"And now you may have your chance," Ms Darbus said.

That caught the attention of Ryan's sister, Sharpay Evans. Her head whipped around. "What?"

Ms Darbus nodded. "Yes! The producers are holding open auditions for teenagers around the country! They'll choose a cast to perform the musical – on Broadway! – for one night only, as a promotional event!"

Sharpay gasped. "This is it!" she said to Ryan. "Our destiny, our fate, our *future* has arrived!" She paused, then added, "*Finally.*"

"Now, before you get too excited . . ." Ms

Darbus held up a cautionary hand. "Hundreds of students will be auditioning. The competition will be fierce!" She relaxed enough to beam at Sharpay and Ryan. "Although I'm sure that East High students are among the most talented – and well-prepared – in the country!"

Sharpay beamed back, knowing that when Ms. Darbus said "East High students" she really meant her, Sharpay, the best actress that East High had seen in . . . well, forever.

Oh, and she meant Ryan, too, of course.

Her hand shot up into the air. "Ms Darbus, what will the producers want us to do for our auditions? Should we prepare a monologue or a dance routine or a song – or maybe all three? And what about costumes? I know we're each allowed just one suitcase, but surely those of us who are going to bring glory and renown to East High should be given an extra luggage allowance? Oh, and what about head shots and makeup and–"

"Somebody should call and warn the producers," Chad muttered to his buddies Troy, Zeke

Baylor and Jason Cross. "They may want to start planning their escape route now."

"Thorough preparation is the sign of a true professional!" Sharpay snapped at him. "Not that I would expect *you* to know anything about being a pro!"

"That's not true," Zeke said.

Chad grinned at him. "Thanks, buddy—"

"Chad is a pro at eating. He can finish off five hamburgers in fifteen minutes!" Zeke finished. Chad shoved him, Zeke laughed and Ms Darbus rolled her eyes. If only she were chaperoning dedicated students like Sharpay and Ryan, instead of all these . . . *basketball* players!

Coach Bolton had had enough run-ins with Ms Darbus in the past to recognize the warning signs of a full-scale tantrum. "Okay, enough with the chatter," he said hastily. "Let's go over the rules of the road again. We're meeting tomorrow at the airport at 6 a.m. Everyone gets to bring one suit-case – *one*. Sharpay, I don't care how many cos-tumes you have – and everyone has to report in twice a day while we're in New York. Also, Principal Matsui wanted me to remind you that—" He glanced down at a paper he was holding. "—'this trip is supposed to be educational, so you should focus on visiting sites of historical and cultural importance.' Is that clear?"

Everyone nodded solemnly, but their eyes were sparkling with excitement. They were going to New York City! With their best friends! What could be better?

The bell rang and everybody burst into the hall, heading for their tutor groups.

"This is going to be a blast!" Troy said to Gabriella Montez. "What's the first thing you want to do in New York?"

"I have to go with Taylor to the television studio in the afternoon," Gabriella reminded him.

His face fell. "Oh. Right. The College Quizmaster Show. I forgot."

"Man, I can't believe you guys actually made it to the finals!" Chad said.

"Well, we didn't have much competition,"

Taylor McKessie said. "Gabriella and I outscored the second place team by fifty points."

"You guys are awesome," Zeke said. "Serious brainiacs. Remind me to call you for tutoring when finals roll around."

Chad shook his head in mock sadness. "Too bad you'll have to study the whole time you're in New York. And Sharpay and Ryan are going to be rehearsing the whole time. Man, I'm glad that all I have to do on this trip is enjoy myself!"

"Seriously," Jason agreed. He flipped open the guidebook that he'd been carrying everywhere for the last month. "What should we do first, the Statue of Liberty or the Metropolitan Museum of Art?"

Chad looked at him as if he'd grown an extra head. "Dude, there's no contest! The number one thing we gotta do is check out Madison Square Garden!"

The other boys nodded. They couldn't wait to see the arena where the New York Knicks played.

But then Zeke said, "What about Little Italy?"

"Madison Square Garden first," Chad said firmly. "Why? What's in Little Italy?"

Zeke's smile lit up the hall. "I have two words for you: awesome pastries."

"Okay, you have a point," Chad conceded. "But basketball comes first. Cookies come second."

"Cannoli," Zeke corrected him. "And don't forget tiramisu!"

As the three boys and Taylor walked down the hall to their next class, still arguing about their itinerary, Troy and Gabriella looked at each other and laughed.

"I think this is going to be the textbook definition of a 'whirlwind tour'," he said.

"Yeah," she said, looking wistful. "I just hope I get to do some fun stuff with you guys."

"You're only going to be on the quiz show for a few hours on Monday," Troy said. "That leaves time for, oh, I don't know. A stroll through Central Park? With pretzels for two?"

Hanging out with Troy was always fun, but hanging out in New York . . .

She smiled at the thought, but then shook her head. "If we win the first round on Monday—"

"Which you will!" he said loyally.

"—then we'll have to go back on Tuesday. And if we win on Tuesday—"

"Oh, right. The finals are on Wednesday. And then we fly home." He hesitated, then admitted, "I know this quiz show is a big deal, but I wish we were going to have more time together."

"Taylor and I may not make it past the first round," Gabriella pointed out. "In which case we'll have plenty of time. . .."

"Hey, you can't think like that!" Troy said. "You guys are unbeatable!"

"I hope so. The grand prize is a college scholarship for each person on the winning team."

"You've got a great shot," he reassured her. "And don't worry. After all, New York is the city that never sleeps, right? We'll have lots of time to have some fun!"

TOP OF THE CLASS

SUPER STUDENT

Test taking can be really stressful. I've put together some study tips for you in the next few pages and Chad has included some, well, less orthodox suggestions. Once you've prepared yourself, there are some great quizzes to test your High School Musical knowledge. But don't worry if you don't get passing marks on your first go - that just means you need to watch the movies and read the books some more, and that kind of homework is fun!

HOW BIG A WILDCATS' FAN ARE YOU?

Are you just a casual fan or a real student of the game? Take this WILDCATS QUIZ to find out how you rate!

1. WHAT DOES SHARPAY'S LICENSE PLATE SAY?

A. PRINCESS
B. FABULOUS
C. DIVA1
D. IMSUPREME

2. WHAT ARE THE WILDCATS' TEAM COLOURS?

A. Red and blue
B. Red and white
C. Black and white
D. Salmon and aqua marine

3. AT LUNCHTIME SOMEONE CONFESSED THEY LIKED TO PLAY CELLO. WHAT GROUP DID THEY BELONG TO?

A. Skateboarders
B. Brainiacs
C. Jocks
D. Custodial engineers

4. WHAT WAS SHARPAY'S MOTHER DOING WHEN SHARPAY CONFRONTED HER ABOUT ALL THE WILDCATS AT THE LAVA SPRING CLUB?

A. Tai chi
B. Gymnastics
C. Yoga
D. Quantum physics

5. WHAT WAS THE NAME OF THE POEM SHARPAY AND KELSI WROTE FOR THE POETRY COMPETITION?

A. "Step by Step"
B. "The Story of Shoes"
C. "Marching to Our Own Beat"
D. "One Good Foot Deserves Another"

6. HOW MANY TIMES DID CHAD'S MUM SEE PHANTOM OF THE OPERA?

A. 25
B. 26
C. 27
D. 24,986

ANSWERS:
1. B
2. B
3. A
4. C
5. A
6. C

Give yourself two points for each correct answer.

If you scored 0-4:
CALL A TO AND REGROUP!
If this were a basketball game you'd be losing by double digits. Getcha head in the game!

If you scored 6-8:
SOUND FUNDAMENTALS
You have a solid grasp of the High School Musical basics.

If you scored 10-12:
SLAM DUNK! GAME OVER!
You are a Wildcat knowledge All-Star and a true champion!

CHAD'S GUIDE TO CRAMMING

I can think of about a thousand things I'd rather do than study but in order to make the grades to stay on the team, studying is a necessary evil. Here are some of my slick shortcuts that might help you, too.

1. Put your study notes under your pillow. It might be hard to believe, but this helps stuff sink in faster. It's called cosmosis or something. And the best part is, you're freed up to dream about fun things, like basketball and girls.

2. Sweet talk. If you're a smooth operator, you might be able to sweet talk the teach into revealing something that's on the test. So work on your chatting skills. But don't be too obvious, because that just ticks them off.

3. Memory aid. This is sometimes called bubonic or demonic or something. Wait...mnemonic, that's it! Anyway, sometimes it's easier to remember things if you can connect it to something else. Example. I was trying to remember who signed the Magna Carta. I knew it was a king but couldn't ever remember the name. So I worked it into a basketball drill. I repeated this in my head at practice: J is for jumper; O is for Overtime; H is for Hang time; N is for Nasty Dunk. King J-O-H-N!

GABRIELLA'S GUIDE TO TAKING TESTS

Check out the A-grader's guide to success.

1. Diet. There are plenty of foods that boost brain power, like blueberries and fish. Also, don't ever take a test on an empty stomach - make sure you have a healthy meal beforehand (so long as it isn't turkey - that will just make you sleepy!).

2. Use colour-coded flash cards to help prepare for the big test. Flash cards might be pretty simple, but they've proven that they can really be a great study aid.

3. Work out a super-strict timetable and stick to it! Here is an example:
Breakfast - short and sweet - 10 minutes.
Revision - 3 hours. Allow for a couple of breaks.
Lunch - Take a longer lunch - 30 minutes.
Afternoon revision - 2 hours. Again, be sure to take a break.
Evening - A good meal and then do something fun to relieve stress!
Before bed - review. This might be a good time to use some of the coloured flash cards again to stimulate the brain. Then make sure to get a good night's rest.

4. Find a revision buddy for the spot tests. It can be discouraging studying alone, but if you have a friend helping, you can motivate each other to keep learning and practising.

5. Whatever Chad told you about sleeping on your notes to increase knowledge osmosis (not fibrosis!) - don't believe him!

HIGH SCHOOL MUSICAL QUIZ

How much do you know about the music and songs from High School Musical and High School Musical 2? Now is your chance to showcase your stuff. Answer the questions and then check to see how well you did at the end.

1. ACCORDING TO "START OF SOMETHING NEW", WHEN CAN ANYTHING HAPPEN?
A. When worlds collide
B. When you take a chance
C. When you least expect it
D. When doves cry

2. WHO SINGS "START OF SOMETHING NEW"?
A. Troy and Gabriella
B. Sharpay and Ryan
C. Taylor and Chad
D. Principal Matsui and Ms Darbus

3. ACCORDING TO "GETCHA HEAD IN THE GAME", WHAT SHOULDN'T YOU BE AFRAID TO DO?
A. To fall on your face
B. To take the hard foul
C. To shoot the outside 'J'
D. To use a loofah in the shower

4. WHO HAS THE MOST TROUBLE 'GETTING HIS HEAD IN THE GAME'?
A. Chad
B. Zeke
C. Coach Bolton
D. Troy

5. ACCORDING TO "WHAT I'VE BEEN LOOKING FOR", WHAT IS IT THAT HAS FINALLY BEEN FOUND?
A. Someone who completes me
B. What I've been looking for
C. That there really is someone for everyone
D. The winning lottery ticket

6. WHO SINGS "WHAT I'VE BEEN LOOKING FOR"?
A. Troy and Gabriella
B. Sharpay and Ryan
C. The Wildcats basketball team
D. Zeke and an oven

7. ACCORDING TO "WORK THIS OUT", WHAT IS THERE NO DOUBT ABOUT SAVING?
A. The summer
B. The whales
C. Ourselves
D. Some sweet moolah

8. WHO SINGS "WORK THIS OUT"?
A. Troy and Gabriella
B. Taylor and Chad
C. Kelsi and Zeke
D. All of the above

9. ACCORDING TO "FABULOUS", THE SINGER NEEDS SOMETHING INSPIRING AND WHAT ELSE?
A. A little fabulous?
B. A lot of things?
C. A little help from my friends
D. A better partner for this song

10. WHO SINGS "FABULOUS"?
A. Troy and Gabriella
B. Zeke and Kelsi
C. Sharpay and Ryan
D. Madonna

ANSWERS:
1.B   6. C
2.A   7.A
3.C   8.D
4.D   9.A
5.B   10.C

TAYLOR'S EQUATIONS

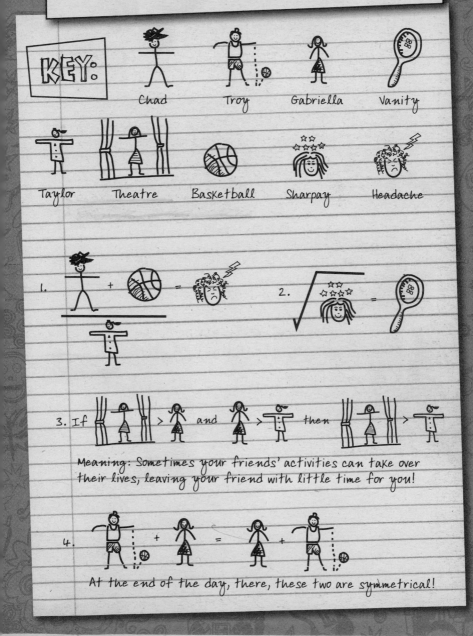

KEY:

Chad • Troy • Gabriella • Vanity

Taylor • Theatre • Basketball • Sharpay • Headache

1. (Taylor + Basketball) / Chad = Headache

2. √(Sharpay + Headache) = Vanity

3. If Theatre > Gabriella and Gabriella > Taylor then Theatre > Taylor

Meaning: Sometimes your friends' activities can take over their lives, leaving your friend with little time for you!

4. Troy + Gabriella = Gabriella + Troy

At the end of the day, there, these two are symmetrical!

PUZZLING PICTURES

How EASILY can you IDENTIFY the students of East High? Take a look at these pictures and see if you know Troy from Taylor and Chad from Sharpay!

This student often helps fellow classmates with their study programs.

This student sees life as one big equation.

This student is the behind-the-scenes talent of Twinkle Towne.

These pictures have got all mixed up! See if you can match the correct heads, bodies and legs together to make four complete characters!

HIGH SCHOOL MUSICAL

ULTIMATE KNOWLEDGE QUIZ

How big a fan are you? Put your knowledge to the test with this Ultimate Quiz!

1. WHAT IS THE NAME OF THE POEM THAT GABRIELLA WROTE FOR THE COMPETITION?

A. "Purity"
B. "Integrity"
C. "Honesty"
D. "Redundancy"

2. WHO ASKED MS DARBUS WHAT HER FAVOURITE SUMMER MEMORY WAS JUST BEFORE SUMMER BREAK?

A. Zeke
B. Jason
C. Gabriella
D. The Ghost of High School Past

3. WHO HAS A SECRET PASSION FOR HIP-HOP?

A. Kelsi
B. Gabriella
C. Martha
D. Principal Matsui

4. WHAT WAS THE NAME OF
   TROY'S SKATEBOARD?

A. Ariel
B. Aurora
C. Belle
D. Jezebel

5. WHAT IS ZEKE'S FAVOURITE MOVIE?

A. The Mask of Zorro
B. The Wizard of Oz
C. Gone With the Wind
D. The Muppets Take Manhattan

6. WHO IS THE GUEST JUDGE FOR THE
   POETRY COMPETITION?

A. Julius Rosenberg
B. Julius Caesar
C. Julius Irving
D. Julius Ibsen

7. WHAT IS SHARPAY'S FAVOURITE DESSERT?

A. Peach cobbler
B. Chocolate éclair
C. German chocolate cake
D. Chocolate ants

8. WHEN WERE THE AUDITIONS FOR TWINKLE TOWNE RESCHEDULED TO?

A. Friday at 3:30
B. Wednesday at 2:30
C. Thursday at 4:30
D. The twelfth of never

9. WHAT KIND OF PIZZA DO TROY AND GABRIELLA LIKE?

A. Barbecued chicken
B. Sausage and onion
C. Pepperoni and pineapple
D. Peanut butter and mango

ANSWERS:

1.C 2.B 3.C 4.A 5.C 6.D 7.B 8.A 9.C

SECRET IDENTITIES

See if you can guess which character is being described by reading the clues below. Write your answers after each series of clues then check to see how well you did by flipping the page when you're done!

A.
1. Currently a Wildcat but considering becoming a Redhawk someday
2. Loves barbecued ribs
3. Taylor claims he has boy disease

ANSWER: Troy

B.
1. Claims he has been behind on homework since preschool
2. Had a crush on Ronda in fourth grade
3. Refers to Sharpay as 'royal blondeness'

ANSWER:

C.
1. Tells Zeke his cookies are "genius!"
2. Sings at a nursing home
3. Offers to clean up the club after the talent show

ANSWER: Sharpay

D.
1. Wins the part of Minnie in a musical
2. Wrote a poem about betrayal
3. Says, "If you act like someone you're not, pretty soon that's who you become."

ANSWER: gabriella

IDENTITIES REVEALED